V

Aura Marquez

Jackie,

You are magic!

Aura Marquez

V

Cover design by: A. R. Redington

Printed in the United States of America

For anyone that has ever been told that they are too much. I took what people deemed as over the top, and turned it into this book. I hope you will do great things with your beautiful traits.

Preface

This book is a love letter to the communities in which I am a part of. To be a Chicana, pansexual, autistic person has not been easy. Growing up I was bullied mercilessly for being different. I wanted to write this book to bring representation to the genre, but even more importantly, I wanted to create a character that was beautiful, strong, and loving, who lives within these communities.

Whenever I tell people I'm autistic more often than not the response is, "You don't look autistic." Our society's understanding of autism is incredibly narrow and skewed. Autism is a spectrum, and the beauty of the people within my community is as varied as the colors in the rainbow. As you read this book, if the way that V acts seems strange or unnatural it's because she does not act in a neurotypical way. V is completely based on me, everything that you see within the book is how my brain works, and how I interact with the world.

Although this book is a work of fiction my hope is that through V's interactions people can see an autistic perspective in an unexpected genre. I don't want to only see autistic representation within books about autism, I want our representation to be as widespread as we are.

Since I enjoy the complexity and intersectionality of life, I have done the same with V's pansexuality. She never has to say that she's two spirit within the novel, just like straight people never have to declare their straightness. Every queer character lives life unapologetically, and fully. One question that has arisen is why I chose to alternate for Madís' pronouns. Madís is based on a few friends that want their he/they pronouns to be used interchangeably. I want this kind of representation to be much more widespread, and I hope that it will lead to more understanding.

Music Playlist Accompaniment

TW: Mention of abuse, drug use, reference to suicide ideation

Chapter 1

I sit on the sidewalk, next to a giant puddle of urine, taking in the sounds of L.A. at night. Sirens, drunken laughter, angry screaming...*God, I love this city.* If I had lived my human life, I would probably be at home right now with a partner and our pets; or maybe I'd be working far into the night at the business I had started. But that's not the life I was meant to live.

I sing "Drip Drops" to myself, one of my favorite **that dog.** songs, as I think. Nobody ever mentioned how mundane everlasting life would be. *I'M SOOOOOOOO BORED.* Everyone's rich, everyone's gorgeous, everyone looks like a teenager—what the hell kind of existence is this? I know a lot of this has to do with being a rich Los Angeles vamp though. The money, beauty, and lust all suck you in and, if you're not careful, you forget there's more to life than status and shallow people at parties.

I felt lazy tonight, and wore a pair of black leggings, a black razor back crop top t-shirt, and my gold hoop earrings. I also never go anywhere without my bright red lipstick, black Loop earplugs, and my black boots. Such a predictable Chicana vamp outfit. At least my pixie cut sets me apart from the others, with my hair short on one side, the top draping over my right eye. Being Chicana with a pixie cut always gets its fair share of opinions. People either love it and tell me I'm brave, or they hate it and start to talk about how much prettier I'd look with long flowing hair. I always respond with, *"Well, it's a good thing you're not me then."*

I get up off the concrete, dust myself off, and start to walk to my favorite club. I had taken a moment to sit and just enjoy the best city in the world, while also feeling sorry for myself, but enough is enough.

As I walk down the street, I can feel heads turning, taking me in, wanting to approach me, but too intimidated to follow through. Being a vamp and picking up humans is like shooting fish in a barrel. Everything about me is designed to attract my prey. As soon as you turn you become irresistible; vampires exude beauty, our scent is filled with pheromones meant to entice, and the sound of our voices pull even the most reluctant human in. We were created to be the ultimate killing machine. It's so easy, it's not even fun.

I remember being human and running into people that looked like they had come out of a magazine, gorgeous, almost too perfect. I look back now and wonder if they were vampires. The good thing is we look so incredibly unattainable that, as much as humans want us, they don't approach us. Otherwise, we'd be chased by human mobs all day. Until I decide I want to talk to a human, I don't have to worry about being harassed. I ignore the looks as I walk by a Thai restaurant filled with hungry patrons. I don't feel like babysitting a human tonight. Then again, do I ever?

Fifteen years ago, this all seemed so exciting. I had been obsessed with vampires since I was in middle school; this special interest is what kept me alive when it seemed like my peers wanted nothing more than to tear me down for who I was. I found comfort in the idea of being so untouchable, so beautiful, so perfectly made to be a predator. A lonely preyed-on girl, wanting nothing more than to devour her assailants for all the pain they caused her.

Learning that vampires existed right before my 40th birthday, as one was literally on the verge of killing me, seemed quite fitting for the little girl who had never stopped dreaming of becoming a monster.

You look at all those vampire shows, novels, and movies, and they tend to focus on the vamps that exist within the 15-25 age range. You never hear about middle aged vampires who've lived half their life as a human, and now must completely change everything they knew and understood about who they are. Yet, here I am, a now 55 year old in a 40 year old's body for life. The funny thing is, I wouldn't trade places with those teenage looking vamps in a second. Having to be treated like a kid their entire existence, going to school over and over again, talk about purgatory! I chuckle as I walk. *Poor bastards.*

I often wonder if that's why I'm so unhappy as a vamp. I got to live 40 years as a human, getting to experience humanity a lot longer than even the oldest vampire I know, before becoming invincible. It's easy to see the difference in vampires who didn't experience humanity for very long, and for the most part I just can't find my place in this world, I didn't really find my place in the world when I was human either though. At least when I was human I did have a few more friends. L.A. vampires are all about money, status, looks and I have all three, but I can't be friends with someone based solely on that. When I'm dragged to vamp events, I comply, and I play their game, but I spend most of the night daydreaming. I wasn't cut out to be vampire royalty, and the fact that I'm constantly being scrutinized by other vamps is exhausting. If I'm in the human world I feel like all eyes are constantly on me, and if I'm in the vamp world I feel like everyone expects something from me. Things just don't ever let up. Nothing like living in a constant state of mild depression.

Is all this worth it? It would be so easy to just end it all...

I'd been so caught up in my thoughts I hadn't realized I'd made it to my destination. I can hear **Bad Bunny's** "Efecto" drifting through the small door of *Shine*, I've been needing this so bad.

I'm ready to get lost in a crowd...to disappear.

Chapter 2

The moment I walk into the club I can smell them. As I move to the dance floor, I don't intend to find the scent that makes my mouth water, and my pupils dilate. I'm not in the mood to deal with humans tonight. I just want to dance, to block out how incredibly monotonous my life is. My entire existence is clouded by my hunger, and when my senses are bombarded by music it's the only time I feel true happiness. "Efecto" blends into "La Hora y El Dia" by **Daddy Yankee, Justin Quiles, and Dalex**. There's a cage off to the side of the dance floor and I'm not going in it, but I put my back against it and let the beat take me. I close my eyes, hold onto a bar with my right hand, and I'm in the zone. I'm bending my knees and sliding down to the floor, letting my hips sway without a care in the world. My left hand pulls my hair back as I bite my lower lip and smile because dancing alone right now is giving me life.

As I'm vibing with the beat, my eyes still closed, someone shouts into my ear, "I love your hair!"

Shit! I wish I could tell them that they could whisper, and I'd hear them perfectly, talk about a buzzkill. Even with my earplugs I can hear people a mile away, but they do help dull the sound. Dealing with sensory processing disorder as a human was challenging, but as a vamp it can be unbearable. I've learned which supports help, and I make sure to use them as much as I need. After years of practice I've found a good balance, so being in a club doesn't send me over the edge anymore.

I roll my eyes, ready to blow them off, and turn to see an incredibly scrumptious human. They're Latine, have short black hair that's shaved on the sides, black tattoos all up their gorgeous olive forearms, big metal rimmed glasses, and the most perfect pink lips I've ever seen. Their face is so angelic that I swear they dropped from heaven (I of course will not say that out loud, it sounds gross and embarrassing). They're the one I was drawn to the moment I walked into this club. I was so busy dancing I didn't realize they'd snuck up on me.

My fangs start to slowly descend (I want to taste every inch of their body), I focus on the beat, I take a deep breath, and force them back. I smile, trying to hide my extreme desire for them. It's so easy to manipulate humans; I could lick their neck without them batting an eye. But I didn't come for this tonight. This is why being around humans sucks (no pun intended).

I start to force myself to focus: *you can't drink, you know you can't*...I look at their lips and respond, "Thank you." I go to turn away and they put their hands on my hips.

"I want to dance with you" they confidently say, while looking me straight in the eye.

Becoming a vampire made eye contact even harder than it was when I was human. It makes my skin crawl since I can see too much of a person's soul. Although some of my autistic traits have become more controllable as a vampire, others are even harder to manage. Eye contact physically hurts me, and with the wrong person it can even make me throw up. So, as they try to look me in the eye I focus on their ear, that's safe...*shit, I want to suck on their ear.* It's so cute, a little nibble couldn't hurt; *focus, focus, you're not here to taste anyone tonight*, I remind myself.

They probably think I'm so weird. How long has it been since they asked me to dance? I respond in my most innocent voice, "That is so sweet, but I'm not looking to dance with anyone tonight." I once again try to turn around.

"Why not? You're an amazing dancer and it doesn't seem as fun to dance alone."

This one is persistent. They must have very high self-esteem to have the guts to approach me and talk to me like this; humans aren't usually this forward. A smile spreads across my face; I don't feel like making them go away, and quite frankly I'm also impressed with their confidence. *As long as I promise not to take them home, I can dance* (I tell myself), *I've totally got the willpower to do that.* "I'll dance, but it can't go any further than that."

"Yea, of course," they reply, but I can hear how drawn they are to me. That kind of heartbeat only occurs when a human's body wants someone so badly, they can hardly contain themselves.

As we move to the music I think, *dang this kid's good!* Our legs alternate and flow perfectly, their hands travel down my back and gently caress me. I close my eyes and continue to dance without a care in the world, loving how the beat reverberates down to my core. I soon realize how much I've missed being touched, intertwined with someone else, forgetting where they begin and I end. I can hear their steady breath and it takes everything in me not to look at them; if I look at them, I'll lose myself and there's no telling what I might do.

The longer I dance with them, the more I realize reggaeton is way too sensual. I need to mix it up or I'm going to kill this sweet young one. I turn to the DJ, "Hey! Can you play some **Selena**?" He gives me a thumbs up and as soon as I hear the familiar start to "La Carcacha," I let out a sigh of relief.

I can always count on music to save me. I dislodge myself from my dance partner and start moving to one of my favorite beats. At this point the mood lightens, my hunger subsides, and I can actually talk again. The crowd is singing and you better bet I am too, "Uno!...Dos!...Tres!...Cuatro!" Fingers in the air and everything. I remind myself that people like to talk, and they like being asked questions. I'm constantly advising myself of expected societal etiquette. Sometimes I don't care if people think I'm being rude, but when I'm with someone I like I try a little harder to follow neurotypical expectations, if they don't stress me out. We're already dancing, knowing a little about them won't do any harm.

"What's your name?"

"Madís[1]...Madís Avila, my pronouns are they and him[2], what's yours?" and they end by winking at me and licking their top lip, *damn they're hot,* I think to myself.

"V, my pronouns are she, her." I'm super unimaginative and V stands for Vampire. When I realized it hurt me too much to use my human name I had to scramble to make a vamp name, V is the only thing that came to mind; I've always been terrible at naming things. After a while it grew on me though, and seemed pretty fitting since I do love things to be literal. I no longer share my human name with anyone; the only vampire who knows it doesn't ever use it, since she knows I can't stand to hear it.

"Come on, what's your actual name?" he asks with a big smile on his face.

"That is my actual name." I answer, annoyance creeping into my voice. I quickly change the subject because I don't want to get into

---

[1] Pronounced Maw-dees (Spanish pronunciation)
[2] Madís is a trans man who goes by they/him pronouns because of this you will see these pronouns interchanged throughout the book (this is explained in the preface).

it. "What ethnicity are you? You're very good at cumbias and most people I meet aren't."

They laugh, "I'm Mexican, my family and I immigrated here when I was little."

I suddenly realize that they do have a small accent. It's incredibly attractive. "That's so cool, I'm Chicana. My parents came here from Mexico too." We both smile; it's always nice to meet someone who, in one phrase, gets where and what you've come from.

"How old are you?" It's hard for me to guess human's ages. I know I haven't been a vamp for very long, but it's interesting how quickly you lose touch with human life.

"I'm 32"

Without thinking I shout, "You're a baby!"

He lifts an eyebrow and asks, "How old are you?"

I, of course give my human age, "40"

"You are not! Come on, tell me how old you really are." He's shaking his head in disbelief at my answer.

"Why is it so hard to believe I'm 40?" I ask as I back away slightly and look up at them with furrowed brows.

"You look like you're in your early 30s. If you're making yourself older than me to scare me away, it's not going to work. Forty isn't old but there's no way you're 40." They're saying all of this, completely unaware that they sound like an idiot.

I'm still dancing but my breathing intensifies as I try difficult not to step onto my soap box. "Well, I am 40, and the only reason you think I'm not is that our society has convinced people, especially women, that aging is bad." I turn away from them, too irritated to look their way. Their comment has hit a nerve and until I tell them what's on my mind I can't dance anymore. I tug at the front of their button up linen shirt and nod my head to the side of the bar.

They slump their shoulders and look uncomfortable, but they follow me. We're wedged between the wall and the corner of the bar when I start speaking again. "Women are told that they need to spend ridiculous amounts of money, time, and energy to stop themselves from aging, and that by the age of 40 they will look like decrepit spinsters if they do not do something about it. I don't look like I'm in my early 30s, I look like I'm 40, and yes 40-year-old women do look this young, beautiful, and hot!" I tried to stay calm in the beginning but by now I'm gesturing wildly, and people at the bar including the bartender are staring at us, wondering if we're in the middle of a love spat. He's dumbfounded, has no idea what to say, and I don't feel bad about putting him in his place. He stands there awkwardly looking down at his dark blue converse and then longingly at the dance floor.

"You still want to dance, or should I just leave you alone?" he bites on his lower lip as he asks. He looks like a puppy that's just been scolded for tearing up a favorite pair of shoes, *damn it, I can't just leave things like this*... I roll my eyes and sigh but grab their left hand with my right and lead them to the dance floor. Even though I've embarrassed them they won't walk away, I'm too irresistible as a vamp.

We continue dancing to cumbias in silence, but the energy is so awkward. I'm about to excuse myself when "La Chona" by **Los Tucanes de Tijuana** comes on and everyone loses their shit. It's a classic, and there's no way I can stop dancing now, so I tell myself that after this dance I'll leave. I start my best quebradita stomps and Madís excitedly shouts, "Damn, you are Mexican!" I laugh because a good song can easily change my mood. With my goth look, people tend to be

16

surprised that I'm so connected to my Mexican roots; it's one of the many things I love to shock others with. This helps to lighten the tension between us and they say, "Hey, I'm sorry about making those comments about your age. I feel really stupid."

"I'm used to people saying stupid shit like that. I hope you learned a little something tonight." I turn away from him but we continue dancing. I like telling people what I think, but I don't hold onto grudges. I appreciate their apology and I get a good vibe from them, but it is a perfect example of how young they are, and how annoying it can be to try to get involved with humans.

After a few more norteño songs, the DJ decides to slow things down with "Ojitos Lindos" by **Bad Bunny and Bomba Estéreo**. As soon as the energy changes Madís is so close to me I can smell his skin, and the pressure of his body against mine makes me salivate. He leans in and says, "I want to fuck you so badly." I'm totally thrown off. I'm used to being that blunt, but very rarely do I find someone else who is. I pull back and look into their eyes. It's not easy to catch me off guard, but Madís just did.

The moment I lock eyes with them I get sucked in and I know I've messed up. I feel an instant connection to them; I can see how hard their family has struggled in this country, and I want their hopes and dreams as much as they do. It's as if our souls intertwine, their heartbeat now becomes what I'm moving to, the music a distant memory.

They slide their fingers into the waist of my leggings and gently stroke my hips and lower back. As I slowly roll my lower body, their hands caress my curves and the heat that's radiating from them makes me wish I could have them here and now.

The club disappears and I see us making love on my bed, our bodies moving just as seamlessly as they do on the dance floor. I can feel the incredible pleasure that comes from their warmth and desire. I taste every inch of their skin, my tongue explores their stomach, its soft flesh making me tingle. They have an Aztec tattoo down the center of their chest, I run my tongue over their nipple and whisper, "You're fucking gorgeous." My fingertips dance over their top surgery scars and then my hand works its way down their side, over their wide hips and across their thigh, I can't wait to feel the inside of them.

I'm still lost in my vision and we're both in complete ecstasy. While my thoughts are clouded by my need for them, I bite into his soft silky neck...*just one little taste*. As his blood enters my system he lets out the most orgasmic moan and I smile as I slowly suck.

I whisper, "I know I make that feel really good, I promise there's more to come." I lower myself and bite his inner thigh, but I've already drank more of his blood than I should have. My heart starts to race, I can't see clearly with him running through my veins. I pull him off the bed and push his body against the wall, I don't realize the hole his skull's left, I don't see his body twitch one last time. The haze fades when I register that his heartbeat has stopped, and his body is lifeless in my arms. I let go and he crumbles to the ground, leaving a trail of blood as he slides down the wall.

I want to scream; I start picking at my skin and force myself not to actually rip it off. I'm suddenly back on the dance floor as the premonition starts to fade...*this is why I can't let myself go, why I can't trust myself*. I start tapping my thumb against my other fingers, *I need to stim more than this,* I realize. *I need to get out of here.*

I've rehearsed this excuse thousands of times, and given it just as many, "I'm too much for you to handle, Baby Boy." I say it with a smile on my lips, but inside I'm breaking.

I can feel his heartbeat drop immediately, the crushed look on his face is too much for me to handle. "You know what? I should get going," I start to walk away, and he grabs my hand.

"I'm so sorry I said that. We can keep dancing; I swear I'll behave myself." Poor thing has no idea it has nothing to do with him.

I look back at him and sadly say, "You did nothing wrong *chulo*[3]. Stay sweet." Then I turn and walk out of the club just as confidently as I walked in.

---

[3] Masculine form of cutie; in Spanish

Chapter 3

"How the fuck do you stay alive?" She teases as she walks out of the nearest alley.

"Shit, you saw all of that didn't you? What the hell are you doing here?" I ask, my exasperation is obvious.

"I happened to be in the club, and got to see that whole little interaction you just had." Mya looks at me with that evil smile she's perfected after years of preying on others, while also gesturing towards the club.

"*Sabes que*[4]? I have my way of being a vamp, and you have yours. I've told you before, mind your own business." We love giving each other a hard time, and we both laugh as I finish this last sentence.

She knows not to push me anymore and we walk in silence. As we stroll down the street I inhale deeply; the smell of L.A. is one of my favorite things: street hot dogs, cigarette smoke, and a hint of garbage. The city is so beautiful at night I hardly miss being out during the day. The red, green, and white neon lights shine in every club. The long lines of hopeful patrons make me smile, I remember eagerly standing in those lines before becoming a vamp. The sound of laughter and dishes clattering floats out of the restaurants that we pass. *Fuck, I love L.A.*

Mya is my only friend– soulmate actually– and although I value her guidance, we do things very differently. Being a vamp has always come naturally to her, and since she's been doing it for 200 years, she's gotten good at it. Then again, from her stories, it sounds as if being

---

[4] You know what; in Spanish

human came easily also. Did being human just come naturally to most people?

Anyway, Mya is so striking you can't help but be infatuated with her. Even vamps lose themselves around her. She's 5'10", was turned at age 25, has a luscious curvaceous body, gorgeous dark caramel skin, and a crown of curly black hair. In case you can't tell, I'm completely in love with her, and although we tried hooking up when we first met, the two of us are NOT compatible romantically. We'd sooner kill one another than ever be sexually intimate again, but there's nothing wrong with thinking your best friend is a goddess who rules the ground she walks on.

"How do you ever expect to dominate this town when you refuse to feed from humans?" She finally says.

"That's the thing, I don't want to control this town. I'm incredibly happy being your lowly minion," I answer as I open my arms and bow before her. She smiles because she loves it when I remind her that she's pretty much my entire world.

"What if you get called to The Commission? You will never have the strength you need to fight." As she says this I can tell her patience is running thin. She's not used to people disagreeing with her. Then again, I also think it's the only reason she can stand me for longer than a night. I challenge her, I push her to be her true self, and even though she acts like she hates it, she secretly craves it.

"If I get called, I'll decide what to do then. Why do I have to live a certain way because there's a chance I could be called to the *dun...dun...dun...COMMISSION.*"

Her nostrils flare and I realize I've taken it too far. It's very unvampire of me to make fun of The Commission. If the elders heard me I'd get quite the talking to. The thing is, I've never been one to play well with others, and being told that I have to risk my life on a commission that keeps order in the vamp world sounds so stupid, I can't help but make fun of it.

Mya stops walking and turns to face me, her hands on her hips, "You know that The Commission is the only thing that keeps rogue vampires in line. Being the highest creature on the food chain takes your ego on a hell of a ride and without an organization like The Commission vampires would have no reason to behave."

I totally feel like a teenager who's being lectured by her mom, and I am so not in the mood for that right now, "I know what you're going to say," I begin, before going into my Mya impersonation: an upper-class L.A. accent, straight back, and head held high, "Now V, don't forget about Jack the Ripper. He fed so often and so much that he couldn't satisfy his hunger for blood. Once humans noticed, the authorities were involved and a frenzy ensued. Our entire way of life was threatened!" I'm pointing my finger at her the way a mother would scold a tiny child and I'm sure I look ridiculous since I have to look up to do this.

I hear a soft laugh at the back of her throat as she throws her head back, "You...are...IMPOSSIBLE. I know this is all a big joke to you, but Jack the Ripper is nothing to scoff at. The way we live now allows us to use humans however we want, live incredibly lavish lifestyles, with very little effort. Some vamps have dreamed of human domination; but the truth is that if those guys took over, the world would turn into a disgusting hellscape, a feeding frenzy, vampires unchecked become ravenous, and are unable to control themselves." Mya loves going on and on about the need to protect our way of life. At this point she's started walking in a circle, her hands are outstretched as she gestures around us to emphasize all that we have.

I know the system is necessary, but I hate being talked to like a child, "I get it, I get it. Jack the Ripper disappeared without a trace and it's all thanks to The Commission. The people of London were able to sleep soundly once again, and vamps stayed under the radar. Such a happy ending, if you completely ignore the fact that vampires continue to rip people apart in secret!" My eyes accusingly look up at her and I'm pouting like a child. We've had this conversation thousands of times and neither of us ever changes our minds.

"Ugh, why do you need to be such a revolutionary all the time?" she screams with exasperation.

My hands begin to gesture wildly as it's now my turn to hop onto my soap box, "Because we have no right to take human lives so that we can live! You know that I hate being like this. That I refuse to go and serve time for The Commission, when their only purpose is to preserve a lifestyle that protects self-indulgent A-holes!"

We're both breathing heavily at the end of this exchange, not because we're actually out of breath but because we're both super pissed, and regret getting into all of this.

I close my eyes and take a deep breath, then another, then another. I take 3 steps towards her so that we're within touching distance, "My love, you know that I'm going to always hate and resent this life. I didn't choose it, and it doesn't fit me the way it does you. I'm sorry for acting like a jerk tonight but that interaction in the club was INTENSE and my nerves are completely on edge. My brain kind of needs to shut off for a while." I run my thumb over her lips as I say this; it's our way of saying, *you know I love you, be patient with me please*.

Her eyes soften and she smiles. After ten years of friendship I know exactly how to appease her, and I'll admit I'm pretty proud of that. Mya blows people off within hours most of the time, so I'm the only one she's kept around this long. As much as I love her, she can be a brat. When you get whatever you want, whenever you want, you forget others do live in this world too. When she gets an attitude I like pulling her back to earth. It's funny how we take turns mothering each other.

I'm also well aware that I hurt her feelings when I talk about how horrible our species is, she's been at it much longer than I have. For the rest of the walk she'll let me retreat into my thoughts so that I can recharge, but I will make sure I apologize once I feel like talking again.

Chapter 4

15 YEARS EARLIER

My breaths come out in jagged gasps, spots cloud my vision, and searing pain consumes me.

"Tsk...tsk...tsk..., this is why you shouldn't have upset me. I wouldn't have had to hurt you if you would have just done what I told you to do. You're so stubborn. At this point I have two options—I let you bleed out in the middle of nowhere, or I turn you. I'm tempted to let you die because you're the only one that's never let me fully control you. Then again, I really love having my children running around the city; you can never have too many vampires in L.A." He calmly says all of this as he sits on top of me, his face over mine. He's a small guy and can't be more than 130 lbs. but I can barely move while he pins me down by my shoulders.

As he's contemplating my fate he looks down at me as if I'm worthless. He bends down and licks the blood gushing from the open wound in my neck. There are no feelings coming from him, I'm about to die and all I can focus on is that he doesn't give a shit that he's about to kill the woman he's been dating. *How could I have been so stupid?*

All of a sudden, he bites into his own wrist and forces it against my lips. I'm gagging, choking on the blood, but he doesn't stop. The metallic goo sticks to the inside of my mouth and coats my tongue. I'm struggling, trying to push him off me, trying to force his wrist away from my mouth but he doesn't budge, his strength is like nothing I've ever encountered.

Finally, he abruptly dismounts me, as my body, tired from fighting, falls against the ground, and rocks dig into my skull. I lay there frozen, disgusted by every part of him. His thick black hair is styled with too much gel. His dark skin reminds me of his betrayal, his ability to use our shared culture to give me a false sense of security. His face that always seemed a little too round, looks bloated and disfigured in this lighting. His perfectly pressed red Armani shirt is now wrinkled and dirty, and I wish I had the courage to spit on it.

He scoffs, "Have fun with my gift." As I lay on my side I see him get into his sports car and drive away. Dirt and rocks fly into my face, and I tightly shut my eyes but even that sends pain down my entire body. I lay on the ground in a fetal position watching my only way out of here peel out in a cloud of dirt. I'm crying, still trying to fill my lungs with air, and I'm ready to die.

I come to a few hours later. *How am I still alive?* The world around me blurs as I try to open my eyes and they hurt all the way to the back of my skull. It's a full moon tonight so although I'm in complete darkness I can make everything out surprisingly well. I frantically look around and all I can see for miles is dirt and patches of weeds, mustard plants, and large boulders. He purposely drove me to the middle of nowhere so that I'd either die or endure an extreme amount of pain while trying to get help.

Every muscle in my body aches, I don't know if I can even stand up. Instead, I get onto my hands and knees, and I start to crawl; I have no idea where I'm going but, even in this state, I know that I can't just lay there. I slowly push myself up to standing and I stagger towards where I think there's a road. I'm covered in dirt and goathead thorns, my hair is full of the dry stems that litter the ground. Suddenly a pair of headlights shine right at me. I shield my eyes against the twin beams that cause a sharp pain from my head all the way down my spine. The car quickly stops and a couple in their late teens rushes out.

The girl runs over to me and puts her right arm around my shoulder to stabilize me. "Robert, we need to get her to the hospital! Ma'am, what's your name? Can you hear me?" Everything is too loud, my brain can't figure out what she's asking me, or how to answer. I slump into her arms and everything goes dark.

Beep...Beep...Beep. The monitor that I'm hooked up to is the first thing my mind registers when I open my eyes. I jolt up in bed. *Diego...I was with Diego...and he hurt me.* My head's pounding and I can't think clearly. I cover my eyes with my hands and coil into a little ball, trying to stop the physical and emotional pain that insists on breaking through. As I sit forward, I feel the sting from the IV in my hand, I've gone too far forward and it's pulling against my skin.

I start to lay back down and a nurse walks in to check my vitals. She has kind eyes and reminds me of my Tia Susana. Her brow furrows when she sees I'm awake. "How are you feeling? Is there anything I can get for you?" I shake my head, still too dazed to talk. "I'll tell Doctor Anand that you're awake."

She walks out after checking the monitors, and an hour later a young Indian doctor walks in. She has beautiful curly hair and the most caring smile I've ever seen. "Hello Ms. Espinoza, do you remember anything that happened?" I shake my head no because I'm still not able to piece together the fragmented memories. "This is going to be hard to hear, but you've been attacked. You were found covered in blood, but there are no wounds. Since you came in unconscious and very weak we decided to admit you and give you some fluids." As she says this next line she scans my body with her eyes. "We can't figure out where the blood came from. Your clothes are torn and it's obvious that there was a struggle. The authorities have been notified and are waiting to speak to you." As she's talking, I become unable to focus, her voice sounds far away, and everything blurs...*VAMPIRE.*

My memories all piece together at once. Diego is a vampire, he almost killed me. While she's still talking, I interrupt her, "I don't want to talk to the police."

"Ms. Espinoza, if you know who hurt you they can keep you safe. I know this is very difficult but..." the doctor is really trying to help but there's nothing she can do for me now. My fate is sealed.

"I don't know who hurt me, and talking to them won't help," I interrupt, "If I'm cleared to go I'd like to leave now please." I'm desperate to get out of here, and I feel a panic attack coming on.

She nods her head reluctantly. She knows I'm lying, but the look in her eyes tells me that I'm not the first battered woman who's refused to get the help she needs. The problem is nobody can help me now.

Doctor Anand has recognized that there's nothing she can say to change my mind and quickly works to calm me down. I can tell she doesn't want me getting worked up in my current state. "It's okay Ms. Espinoza, we're not going to make you do anything you don't want to. I'm here to help, I promise. I will get your dispatch papers. If you need anything I am always here...please come and look for me."

"Thank you, doctor." As I sit waiting I pull my hair over my face and breathe it in deeply, my hands work through it over and over again. I stay like this until I'm given my dispatch papers; I get dressed and take an Uber home. I live in a converted garage that's detached from the main house. It's freezing in the winter, boiling in the summer, full of cockroaches, but it's the only thing I can afford in L.A. right now, so it's home.

I collapse onto the floor as soon as I walk in and start to shake, then I start to gag, heaving in waves. The retching is so uncontrollable, I feel like I can't breathe at times. *He was a vampire, and he didn't kill me, he turned me. Vampires really exist, they fucking exist, and one almost ripped my throat out tonight.*

I've read every vampire book you can think of since I was a teenager, so I know exactly what all of this means, if the literature was accurate. He had completely stripped the flesh off my neck and shoulder, but with his blood in my veins, I had healed by the time I got to the hospital. In 24 hours I will be consumed by the thirst for human blood, and if I don't feed, I'll die. I can no longer go out during the day. Today's my last day as a human.

I sit there stunned. As a kid this was my wildest dream, and a week before my 40th birthday it's my biggest nightmare. I know what's going to happen to my body during and after. I know what I'm about to become, and I have no idea how I'll handle any of it long-term. I've seen this go sideways in hundreds of shows, movies, and books, so first thing's first: I need to feed soon, before the hunger consumes me.

Since vampires have been my special interest for over 25 years I've fantasized about what I'd do if this ever happened, even though I didn't know vampires actually existed. My special interests hold a big space in my brain. My vampire fascination consisted of me thinking of scenarios and worlds in which vampires were real. I'd daydream about them for hours; it was one of my favorite escapes as a teen. My peers didn't look kindly on this. We were many years away from Twilight

29

bringing vampires into mainstream popularity, so I was just the super creepy kid who wouldn't stop talking about monsters. *Joke's on them!* Now this knowledge is going to help me survive.

I must say I am taking the fact that the guy I was dating is a vampire— and that I will be one soon— quite well. We'd only been dating for 4 months, but the hold he had on me was so strong I felt as if I had loved him forever. Deep down, maybe I knew that vampires did exist, or at least wished they did. Truth be told, what Diego did to me and the way he treated me hurts much more than the realization that vampires are real. As I recall his name, a chill runs through me. *What a low life—* and I'm sure he was one far before he started drinking blood.

Oh shoot, I'm getting lost in my thoughts, I realize. I look at the clock; 4:00 AM, it's too close to sunrise. Once I drink, I don't know how I'll react to sunlight, and I don't want to risk it. I get under the covers and try to pull my weighted blanket over me, but every inch of my skin hurts. I use a sheet instead, trying to push everything that's just happened out of my head for the night.

Later that day...

I wake up at 8 PM as the last rays of light are leaving the garage. My head's pounding, my eyes burn, every sound makes me cringe, and my skin stings when my clothes brush up against it. This is beyond anything I've ever experienced with my sensory processing disorder. My sensitivity has been turned up 100%; it must be part of my body changing. I crawl out of bed and pull on a long black midi dress and step into black flats, the closest things I find on the floor.

I leave the garage and head to my car, which I had parked blocks away because L.A. parking is horrible. With every step my bones ache. I finally get to my black Honda Civic, slide in, and start driving to the worst bar I've ever been to: Star Lounge. The type of guys that go there have no respect for women at best and can actually be pretty dangerous at worst. Women who know the bar/club scene are aware never to step foot in that place. My first meal is sure to be there.

As I'm driving, I stream "Personal Jesus" by **Depeche Mode** to get in the right headspace. I can't believe I'm about to do this. I walk into the bar and sit at a dark table. I love people watching and I do this for fun on a regular basis. I have my headphones on because the sounds are overwhelming. Even when I wear my headphones, if I focus on a couple, I can make out their conversation perfectly. People have joked that I have superpowers, but I laugh and say, "Nope, just my disability." I use this skill often, and it's one that I'm fond of, as long as I have my headphones or earbuds at all times; without them, noise will trigger an anxiety attack pretty quickly.

I can see every interaction in the bar, on the dance floor, at the different tables. As I'm observing, I notice exactly what I was looking for. A guy with a black goatee stands next to a girl whose back is to him and casually drops something into what I presume is her drink. *Gotcha.*

I walk up behind him and tap him on the shoulder. He turns around as if he's been caught, but when he sees that it's just me, he relaxes and smiles. He thinks I have no idea what a scumbag he is. "Hey! Would you want to head out to the back with me? I'm looking for a good time." I make my shy little girl's eyes and look up at him.

He's salivating at this. "Sure honey, whatever you want."

As he's walking towards the door, I bump the glass and spill the liquid he'd roofied. We walk out of the club and head to the back of the building where the dumpsters are kept. It's dark, empty, and overlooks a small parking lot. He pushes me up against a brick wall forcefully and starts to pull my dress up, "You're a pretty little thing." His breath is rancid and the energy coming off him makes me sick to my stomach. Although his energy makes me queasy, the pulsing vein in his neck triggers something within me. I feel a tearing sensation at the top of my gums and can feel my fangs slowly descending. My vision also changes, my periphery has expanded, and I can see all around without moving my head and although there's only a dim light bulb above us, I can see everything very clearly. This transformation sends a searing pain through my skull, but my thirst overshadows it. *I need blood, and I need it NOW.* I hold my breath and quickly kiss his neck so that I don't have to touch him for too long; I sink my teeth in as hard as I can and start to drink.

"Owww, get off of me bitch!" he screams, trying to push me off, but I just bite harder and continue to drink. As his blood enters my system, I feel invincible, his life force repairing my muscles, strengthening my senses, transforming me. Before I know it, he's gone limp. I let go and he falls to the ground.

"That's what you get, asshole," I'm pretty sure he's dead but I don't care; I'll feed off jerks like him any day. I wipe the blood that's trickled from my lips with the back of my hand and walk away. I'm not too worried about hiding the body; people turn up dead in L.A. all the time. This is also a freaky city and it's not like Diego and I are the only vamps here, I'm sure the bite marks won't seem odd to the mortuary.

Even if they do I doubt they'll even find me, this dirt bag has probably been out here plenty of times with a ton of women.

My mind races the entire drive home. I'm *a vamp, I'm a vamp!* I feel strong, powerful, eternal. I've dreamed of this all my life, and now I get to live it. Diego was a disgusting piece of shit but he gave me everything I've ever wanted. I get home and tuck myself into bed with a big smile on my face. *Everything's going to be different. Everything's going to change.*
I can't wait.

That day, my dreams are interrupted by nightmares. Diego's face as he screams at me, touches me without my consent, tells me I'm a worthless whore. The putrid smell and taste of that pervert in the club overloads my system. I wake up dry heaving, my eyes full of tears. I clasp my hands over my mouth so that I don't scream. The walls in this place are thin and I don't want my housing providers to hear me.

I get out of bed, start to pace, and write in the air. Any phrases that pop into my head become invisible handwriting flowing from my finger. The stimming helps and I start to calm down. *It's understandable that I'm going to be traumatized, it will take time to heal, it's okay.*

As I start to relax and feel more grounded, I realize that the world is different. I look up because I can hear every single sound outside of my garage– cars honking, people laughing, cats fighting. I'm used to the sounds of the city, but instead of faint background noise it's as if they're inches from me. I run to my purse and pull out my earplugs. As I put them on, everything is quieted to a whisper. *Much better.* I exhale as the silence starts to calm my nerves.

I look out the window and notice that I can see every detail of my neighborhood, I can see my neighbor's dog taking a shit in his front yard, eight doors down in complete darkness. *Wow, this is amazing.* I wonder about all those other vamp abilities I've read about. Keeping my earbuds in, I pull on some black sweats, a yellow t-shirt, and my grey *You Are Valid* rainbow sweater[5]. I head out the door and start walking to my car. *I have an idea.*

I drive to a park that I would have never stepped foot in after dark as a human. I go to the far end and run as fast as I can to the other side, spanning about a mile in two seconds. *That was so exhilarating, oh my gosh!* Then I look for the tallest tree I can find, walk up to its base, and jump with as much force as possible. I end up at the top branches! *This is badass, I'm like a superhero!* Should I fight crime? What does one do with all this strength?

As I drive back home, I realize something; I can't go to work anymore. I'm the office manager of a real estate firm, but I can't go out into the sunlight. *Shit, what am I going to do?* I start wracking my brain, but anything that I could do would be during the day. I used to be a personal assistant for someone famous and I lived in a nice apartment, had good money, but after a while it wore on my mental health. I decided to quit, rent a shitty place that was cheap, and try to figure things out. The real estate job is okay money, and low stress, so I was planning on staying there until I started my own social media consulting business, where my real passion is. I know it sounds silly, but I love social media algorithms; I'm able to figure out how they work easily, and nowadays people will pay a lot for that kind of thing; I'd just always been too scared to take that risk. Now that I can only work at night, what do I do?

---

[5] Real sweater can be purchased from megemikoart.com

How do other vamps make it work? Diego was loaded, but he never told me what he did for work, and I only saw him at night; now I get why. I was also so obsessed with him that I didn't ask any questions. Thinking back, other than being rich he had nothing going for him. He wasn't good looking (I guess not every vamp's going to be hot), he had a horrible personality, he wasn't even very smart. Was he controlling me with some kind of vampire mind control? No wonder he'd get so mad when I wouldn't do what he said sometimes. I must have been partly immune. As I think about him a shiver runs down my spine and I feel like I want to throw up. What a disgusting sorry excuse for a boyfriend.

I get to my neighborhood and park as close as I can to my house, which is the usual three blocks away. As I'm walking home I notice that I don't really need to breathe anymore. I do because I'm used to it, but if I stopped nothing would happen. *Just another quirk of being undead, I guess*? Once I get into my garage I start pacing, pulling on my hair, and trying to get this all figured out. I start taking deep breaths before remembering that I don't need them, but it's such an ingrained support that the action still calms me down.

After some verbal stimming, I head for the round mirror that's over my dresser, realizing I haven't checked to see if I look any different. I'm still me but my skin looks radiant, my light brown eyes almost sparkle, and my features seem more pronounced. I also notice a few myths right away. Despite the idea that vampires are white, my skin is still a beautiful honey color. Obviously, I also notice that I can see my reflection perfectly, and I'm still wearing the cross I got for my first communion. As time goes on I'll just have to keep trying things out to see what's make-believe, and what my new existence really allows me to do.

I lay on my bed and look up at the ceiling. It's the original garage ceiling with exposed beams and I love tracing the wood grains with my mind. I grab my weighted blanket and now that I'm not in pain I can lay it over me. I hug my Stitch stuffy, that's always on my bed, and squeeze it while I try to start figuring things out.

I've heard a bunch of friends say that waitressing and bartending make good money. I don't know anything about alcohol— never touch the stuff— but I did work in a cafeteria in college. I can work at a nice restaurant and make extra in tips while I get this all sorted out. I'm sure there are tons of other ways that vampires make money; I just need time to get to know this new world better.

I start to tuck myself into bed, but since I'm feeling really jittery I put on my headphones and turn on my playlist. The first song that comes on is, "Where Does the Good Go" by **Tegan and Sara.** Its sweet melody calms me down and I drift off to sleep.

The next night...

I've always loved wearing black. I wonder if it goes back to wishing I could disappear when I was in middle school. Whatever the reason it makes me feel safe, and even though I've tried going out of my comfort zone when I shop, I always end up in the black clothing section.

Since drinking that guy's blood I feel amazing, no more pain, my skin doesn't hurt, my eyes don't burn. I still wear my Loop ear plugs because, without them, my vampire hearing is way too much to handle.

All of this makes me excited to start my new life. I get my resume and cover letter and head to a fancy restaurant that had a hiring ad online. I do not park with the valet because this place is money, and I can't afford to spend it right now. Standing in front of the *Evergreen* sign, I take a deep breath– again, out of habit versus actual need– before heading in. This is the nicest restaurant I've ever been in. I've always been more of a hole in the wall restaurant, food truck enthusiast. I never felt comfortable in posh places like this, and I'm not a huge fan of super fancy food either.

I ask to speak to the manager and as I'm waiting for the hostess to come back, I'm taking it all in. The walls are a sage green color with an ombre effect that turns lighter as it works its way up to incredibly high ceilings. Everything in here has an organic feel to it despite the clean lines and minimal design. The chairs and booths are rounded. The chandeliers are strange amorphous black blobs made of glass.

I'm still lost in my observations when the hostess returns. "Follow me, he's really busy, but very eager to speak to you as we're incredibly understaffed."

The kitchen is frantic. "Denise, check on table nine. I think they're still missing a plate! Daniel, hurry up, these orders have been sitting here too long!" I've been standing next to the manager silently waiting for him to walk me into an office, or at least out of the kitchen, when he quickly turns to me and says, "You know what sweetie, we just had another person quit today, you look pretty normal." He inspects me one last time for good measure. His eyes scan my pixie cut down to my black boots and then makes his final decision. "You're hired. I'm going to have you work in the kitchen until you get to know the menu."

He's in a rush and there's no time for formalities, so as he's talking a mile a minute, I'm taking all of it in, nodding and trying to hide my excitement. *Oh my gosh, I got the job!*

They're so strapped for workers that I head to the back and get to work right away. It's Friday night and the restaurant is packed, the back is chaotic, but because of my vampire abilities I love the fast pace. It's physically demanding, but I don't get tired. I'm a hard worker and a fast learner. I immediately get along with all of the cooks from the moment I start talking to them in Spanish, there's a collective "OOOHHHHHHHH!" As they raise one hand with whatever kitchen tool they're holding. I love being around *mi gente*[6]. After the first night I can tell I'll do well here, and I rest easy knowing that I'll at least be able to pay my bills.

At the end of the night I go home, take a hot shower, and slide into bed thinking to myself, *I'm going to be alright.*

One week later...

I've been waitressing at *Evergreen* and I don't hate it but so many customers are such assholes. I have a good memory and am able to memorize conversations word for word, so taking people's orders is a piece of cake but you wouldn't know that by how they treat me. I soon realize that working in the back was way better than the front, but I didn't make tips working with the cooks. The customers are a bunch of rich pricks who think that everyone was put on this earth to serve them. I'm constantly having to bite my tongue when I talk to them.

Tonight, a crotchety old man called me sweet lips and grabbed my ass, right in front of his stupid, enabling wife. Vampires are

---

[6] My people; in Spanish

supposed to have the ability to use mind control, that's what Diego did to me after all, so I look him straight in the eyes and say, "Apologize and never touch me again."

He starts to laugh hysterically and- shockingly- so does his wife. "We've got a fiery one tonight Margaret! Should we take this one home?" *Oh shit, it didn't work, maybe that power only exists for certain vampires...*

Crap, well at least the old pervert found it funny. It takes all my self-control not to rip his throat out then and there. I can't afford to lose this job, I barely have enough to pay my bills as it is. I smile and quickly walk away, hoping that I can trade tables with one of the other servers.

The rest of the night runs like every other: busy, crappy tips from the ones that look like they have the most money, condescending stares, and rude treatment. I constantly daydream about going all "Carrie" on everyone in this restaurant. Bathing myself and feasting on their million dollar blood- 'cause according to the way they act- it must be way better than anyone else's. Unfortunately, I have to keep it together the way I always have, while they get to act like they own the world.

As I'm picking my stuff up from the back room one of the waitresses comes up to me, "Hey, V, we're all headed to Sylvester's bar for drinks tonight, want to join?"

I think for a second, a night out would be nice, but I'm not in the mood for a bar. "That sounds really fun, count me in next time, I'm just going to head home."

"No problem, don't let those stuck-up dicks get you down, ok?" And she winks as she walks away.

39

As I'm driving home I realize I do need a break. I didn't feel like being around people I know, but being around strangers sounds very enticing right now. I run into the garage, change into a black bodysuit, black leather skirt, ankle boots, and rush back out to my car. As I head to my favorite club, *Shine,* reggaeton beats are already playing in my mind.

I walk in, and close my eyes, letting the rhythm move me, and with my new vamp powers I can sense humans without even looking; maneuvering to the dance floor is no big deal while I let myself get lost in the music. I have my earbuds in because this amount of noise would have made me completely unable to function, and they mute enough to make it bearable. "BESO" by **ROSALÍA** and **Rauw Alejandro** starts to play and I notice the most delicious guy I have ever seen from across the dance floor.

I walk over to him and he's feeling me just as much, he can't take his eyes off me, and a knowing smile spreads across his lips as I stride over to him. I put my hand behind his neck and pull him towards me. With my right leg in between his thighs, our hips start swaying to the beat. I take his hands in mine and lift them above our heads then slowly lower them behind my back.

He's so appetizing, I could devour him on the dance floor right now. His facial hair frames and compliments a strong jawline. My fingers long to tousle his black curly hair, and I can practically taste his olive skin. As we're dancing, I lean in and kiss him. While I seductively suck on his bottom lip and then gently nibble, his hands roam my body desperately, he can't get enough of my soft curves. I whisper in his ear, "Do you want to go to the bathroom?" He breathlessly nods yes. I place his right hand on my shoulder and I escort him to the back of the club. I can feel his eyes on my ass as my hips sway while I strut.

The lock barely clicks and I press him up against the wall. I'm kissing his neck, while he hikes my skirt up. I wrap my right leg around his hip, and he grabs my outer thigh with his left hand as I moan. His right hand tickles my inner thigh as it works its way up and slowly starts to stroke the inside of me. I skillfully unbutton his shirt, every inch of him is such a turn on I almost orgasm just by looking at his body, and the fact that he's good with his fingers doesn't hurt either.

He has tattoos all over his chest and shoulders, *FUUUUUUUUCK he's hot.* Over his right pec is a tiger over the Puerto Rican flag with a tribal vine running towards his back. The left side is the Devil Dog on top of the Eagle, Globe, and Anchor. Oh my gosh, he was/or is a Marine, now I'm imagining him in his uniform... My fangs slowly descend as I get closer and closer to climaxing.

Humans are extraordinary. I start to kiss and trace his tattoos with my tongue. I work my way down his chest and kneel at his waist. As I'm licking his hip bone, I start to unbutton his pants.

All of a sudden, I start to feel the hunger, building from a low rumble to an all consuming screech from the pit of my stomach. This need quickly and completely consumes me, overpowering and replacing my arousal. I work my way up to his neck and bite; unlike my first victim he exhales and pulls me in closer. But just as his blood starts to flow into my mouth, something else happens.

I'm transported. Suddenly, I'm seeing hundreds of images at once- his entire life flashing before my eyes- and every emotion tied to each memory is hijacking my senses. My system is overloaded, making it impossible to form a conscious thought, the overstimulation making it

41

impossible for me to control my actions. I continue to drink on instinct, both feeding on his physical blood and craving his life, his connections, his humanity. I want to take it all in, and I can't stop.

I hear someone banging on the bathroom door and it breaks me from my trance. I wake to see that he's lifeless in my arms. Although he still has a pulse, it's very weak. I drape his arm around me and open the bathroom door. Luckily, his weight is no match for my vamp strength, making it easy to wind through the crowd, and toss him into the car. I rush this stranger-turned-meal to the hospital. After knowing all of his private feelings and thoughts it's the most heinous betrayal when I leave him laying at the double doors to the ER of Cedars-Sinai Medical Center. I go home, lock the door, and get under the covers. Hugging my knees to my chest, I rock back and forth, and hum. *What did I just do? I may have killed someone, someone good, and beautiful, I may have ended his entire life. Are other vampires like this? Where did I go? What were those visions?* I don't understand any of this and I don't know any vampires, so I have no idea how I'll figure this out.

Suddenly, I remember something that has nothing to do with vampires...my Mama Azucena's[7] gift. Ever since I was little I'd had the ability to understand people at a deeper level than anyone else. I could look at someone and tell if they had good or bad intentions. If someone was in a bad headspace, I could see the energy around them. It would even mess me up sometimes; I'd encounter someone that was hurting so bad that their feelings, their energy, would suck me in. I'd have to go home and sleep, or I'd fall into a deep depression. My mom used to say, *"Tu Mama Azucena y yo éramos así, ahora puedo ver que tú también lo*

---

[7] One way to refer to a grandmother in Mexican culture is to add Mama to the front of their name.

tienes[8]." After a while I got used to my gift and learned how to live with it, but it took years of practice. Whatever happened in that club was like my gift but magnified; my vampire abilities must have morphed it. The only way I learned how to control it as a human was with my mom's support. *How will I ever learn to control this?* I'm all alone now.

If that's what it's like when I feed from people, I can never risk feeding from anyone that I don't want to hurt. I killed that first man, but he was so horrible that I didn't care, and I didn't notice that I had lost control once I was feeding. I enjoyed the anger and hatred that I felt while I fed on him. At the time, I thought they were my feelings, but looking back I think I was channeling his feelings.

I'll have to make sure I only feed from people that deserve it because there's a good chance they won't live after I'm done with them. Shit, I didn't think it would feel this horrible to feed. If I didn't hate Diego so much I'd reach out to him for answers, but I'd rather rot in this garage than come in contact with him again.

I've got to keep my head down, feed only when necessary, and just take it day-by-day. Other than the waitressing I still haven't figured out how else I'll make money, so I'll just stay there until I get it all worked out. If others have figured this out it shouldn't be that bad. I'm sure I'll get the hang of it.

---

[8] Your Mama Azucena and I were like this, now I can see that you also have it; said in Spanish.

Chapter 5

"Excuse me! Miss! I did not order this! Can you believe this waitress? She's a freaking moron! I thought *Evergreen* is supposed to be one of the best restaurants in the city, it has horrible service if you ask me. Miss...I...OR-DER-ED...THE...FI-LET...MIG-NON." She says this last part as loudly and slowly as possible to emphasize her belief that I don't speak English very well.

"I'm sorry, my mistake. I will take it back and make sure you get your correct order," I answer with the fakest smile I can muster plastered on my face. *Bullshit! She ordered the branzino. I have a fucken photographic memory!* I even remember her pointing to it on the menu while overenunciating to make sure I understood her then, too. Rich bitch just didn't like it once it came. She has the money to pay for it, but humiliating me is a bonus on top of getting her free meal I guess. I go to the back and yell at the cook, *"Rodrigo! La pinche babosa que ordenó el pescado dice que quiere filet mignon[9]."* I can hear him cursing under his breath. *Rich people are the worst.*

I turn to the other waitress, "Nancy, I'm going to take my break now. Watch out, the lady at table seven is a bitch." I go out into the alley and sit on my favorite crate, inhaling the smell of garbage, it's so soothing. It's the opposite of this bougie restaurant, and I welcome it.

---

[9] The fucking dumbass woman that ordered the fish says she wants filet mignon; said in Spanish

"What the hell am I doing here? I'm a freakin vampire. Then again, getting turned by a sociopath and having no one to teach me how to vamp didn't exactly set me up to thrive in this life. I've been trying to figure this out on my own for the last five years, and nothing." I'm talking out loud, pacing, and hitting my palms together because I'm really wound up right now and my brain needs to stim and verbally process before I go back in. "I don't know how to mind control humans, I don't get how other vampires are so rich, and I can't feed without killing people. To top it all off, thanks to gentrification, I'm not sure how much longer waitressing will pay the bills." I throw my head back in exasperation.

"Uuuugggghhhhh! One day I'm going to snap and kill everyone in the restaurant if I don't figure all of this out. I can't live like this for eternity! Why is everything always so hard? Why can't I just get the way things work? If an imbecile like Diego figured this all out, why can't I? Chill V, chill… He had support. He had disgusting vamp friends just like him. I've realized now that part of his 'gift' to me was that he was leaving me to figure this all out alone. I hate him so much! What an ASSHOLE!"

I'm interrupted by the back door opening "V, your break is up. Were you yelling? Are you okay?"

"I'm fine, just having a bad day." I close my eyes and take three deep breaths.

"Well, the locals are getting rowdy." That's our code word, and it snaps me out of my fit. I open my eyes and Nancy and I smile conspiratorially. When the rich clientele get super extra, we like to get a little extra with their food. Funny how snobby people don't realize that you shouldn't treat people like trash, especially people who control the most intimate parts of your life.

I take a deep breath and head back in. Back to the humiliation, to serving people that think they're better than me, and feeling like a complete failure. As I walk into the restaurant ready to put on my, "Yes ma'am" face, the hair on the back of my neck stands up. I notice the most beautiful young Black woman I've ever seen. Her smooth dark skin looks like silk, and her supple lips make me lick mine with desire. Without thinking I mouth, "Holy shit." She smiles. Oh my god, she saw that!

As the shock of seeing her starts to wear off, I realize she's a vamp. I can smell the power exuding from her and I'm drawn to it, like a moth to a flame. She's a freaking vamp! *So, I've just humiliated myself in front of the most regal vamp I've ever seen, cool, cool.*

I walk over to her table, pretending I didn't just make a complete fool of myself. "Good evening, my name is V, and I will be your server tonight."

She laughs, "That's so original." Oh my gosh she's mocking me. "Who's your mentor cutie?" She thinks I'm such a joke, but I think she may be flirting with me too. Dang, I really hope she's flirting with me.

"I... I don't have one." If I had the ability to blush I'd be bright red right now, I must sound like such an amateur to her.

"That's what I thought. Let's go, you're coming with me." She picks up her purse and starts walking out. I just stand there stunned; I can't leave in the middle of a shift. What is going on right now? I look around to see if anyone is looking at me, at her, but they're all going about their normal business.

She turns around, shocked that I'm not at her heels, "I said it's time to go." As if I'm in a trance I quickly walk up behind her and follow her out the door. She gives the valet one look and her black hypercar is there within seconds. Damn, this vamp knows what she's doing. I get in the car immediately. She's playing **Rihanna's** "Stay" as she weaves in and out of traffic. I have no idea where we're going but she's so intoxicating, I don't care. If she drove me off the edge of a cliff, I'd be all in.

We drive up to a mansion in Coldwater Canyon. As she parks, someone runs to open her door. I just sit there staring at her as she gracefully slides out. She struts to the door and smiles over her shoulder, "It's time to enter Oz, Dorothy." *Oh shoot, I'm supposed to be following her.* I fumble with the passenger door, try to get out quickly but trip on the toe of my boot. She softly chuckles; even though her back is to me, she knows exactly what just happened.

I'm the clumsiest vampire in the history of vampirism. I used to trip over my own two feet and walk into things all the time as a human, my brain just has a hard time with spatial awareness. Since becoming a vamp it only happens when I'm really nervous. If my mind has too much to process at one time something's gotta give, and that something is usually my sense of coordination. I can't believe I keep embarrassing myself in front of this vamp. If I wasn't so alone I would have left her driveway right then and there, but I have nothing, no one. I can't walk away from this.

As I cross the threshold of her house my jaw drops, I'm frozen; this is the kind of place I've only seen in movies. My celebrity ex-boss didn't have a home that was this impressive. Everything is a cool white. The modern construction is an open floor plan with every room flowing into the next, and incredibly tall, vaulted ceilings. It doesn't look like any surface in this house has ever seen a speck of dust, but as immaculate as it is, it doesn't feel unwelcoming. I love it. An entire wall is made of windows that look out into the city. *The City of Angels.* There are bouquets of fresh white roses everywhere and the smell is just as enchanting as this vampire.

I just stare out, completely mesmerized by this place, this woman. *This vamp.* I slowly turn to look at her again and realize her eyes have been trained on me this entire time. "I never get tired of seeing a young vamp come into my world for the first time. I'm Mya by the way."

I don't even know how to start, there's too much running through my head and I can't decide what to say first. I just stand there gawking at her, like a damn fool. In my defense, I tend to go nonspeaking when I get overwhelmed, but this is beyond that. I don't even feel worthy to be standing in her presence. I can tell she's much older than me, even though her young appearance wouldn't be questioned by any human. What does one say to the most majestic creature they've ever seen?

"Your house is beautiful," I manage to choke out. *Oh my gosh, that is so basic.*

She giggles softly, "I haven't met a vamp as lost as you in a long time. I don't usually take on projects, but I couldn't leave you to waitress. You're so pathetic, it's cute." She gives me a pouty face and her pity makes me cringe. Damn, she cuts deep.

Her last comment sparks a fire in me and I'm able to slightly break her spell and find my voice. "I may be pathetic, but I'd take that over being arrogant any day."

"You do have a spine! Oh good! I was starting to think I'd been wrong about you." As she says this she slowly walks towards me. Her scent is overwhelming. My mouth starts to water, but not the way it does with humans. I want her, I want every single part of her. My eyes hungrily take in her voluptuous breasts and her perfect, round hips. *Damn she's sexy as hell.*

She realizes what she's doing to me instantly. "I'm so sorry! I have that effect on some vamps, and all humans. Each of us has our own strengths, and mine is manipulating desire. I can usually tell when I affect someone, and I'm able to tone it down, but you're a bit of a wild card. Harder to read than expected, I didn't think you'd react." Even though she's apologizing I can tell she loves what she just did to me, her eyes glisten, and she looks me up and down while biting her bottom lip.

As soon as she speaks it feels as if a veil has been lifted; although I can still see how beautiful she is I'm no longer paralyzed by my need for her. *Fuck! I would have done anything to please her. What must it be like to have that kind of power? Can she teach me to do that?*

I hope she lets me stay. Not only do I desperately need her guidance, but I've never felt so drawn to another person in my entire life. Her vampire gift isn't controlling me anymore but I still want her more than I've ever craved anyone. This is beyond lust or infatuation, I never believed in love at first sight, but I'm pretty sure I'm experiencing it right now.

Chapter 6

PRESENT DAY

"You've been so moody lately! Come with me to today's party. You know I usually leave you alone, but you've been extra sad and I can't stand to see you like this," Mya pleads as she cleans the kitchen counter. When I met her years ago, I figured that this place was spotless because she has a fleet of workers, it turns out she does most of the cleaning herself; it calms her. I'm super messy and I know it's a huge pet peeve of hers so I try to keep my spaces in decent condition in order to respect the fact that she's let me live here long-term.

"Whose party is it?" I drop my head on the kitchen table and unhappily groan after asking.

"It's one of the elder's, he just turned a new partner, it's her introduction to the masses, yada, yada... you get it."

"Ugh, you seriously want me to attend that shit? You know I hate ALL of those people." I pick my head up and start tracing the veins of the wooden dining room table, a sour look plastered onto my face.

She pauses her cleaning and looks up at me with a knowing glance, she never forces me to go to vamp events and she's trying to figure out how far to push me. She tilts her head as she examines me and instead of saying anything looks down and continues to scrub.

The kitchen is the room I think fully represents Mya. The walls, tile, and countertops are a pristine white. The cupboards are a deep dark wood, they were repurposed from a 200-year-old church, Mya is very proud of that for some reason. There are very few walls in her house. The "wall" next to me is made up of large glass panes and looks out onto the pool and hot tub area, which is decorated like a secret garden. Roses, wildflowers, and vines cover the outer portion of the concrete that frames the pool. The kitchen leads right into the living room, which is my favorite room. One of my preferred activities is cuddling with Mya on our huge, comfy, white velvet couch and binge-watching Netflix; I'm such a homebody.

I've always hated cooking but the fact that I can feel every part of Mya's natural beauty and simplicity- the part of her that no one knows of- makes the kitchen my second favorite place to hang out.

"That human from the club-Madís-really got into my head. I've been so off since that night." Even now, as I say this to her, I can't focus. It's like I can taste him, but other than dancing and the vision, nothing else happened! "There's something I haven't told you about that human. I didn't want to say it out loud because it would make it real. They're a soulmate."

Mya closes her eyes and then slowly looks up at me, "Baby, I'm sorry."

"Whatever, with everything I saw in his eyes, and how I feel about him I can never be near him again. It's too tempting, and I don't trust myself." Ever since I was little I've had this ability to detect my soul mates, and it's not the one person for the rest of your life narrative that most imagine. When I meet certain people it's like my soul recognizes them, something inside of me awakens and is tied to them instantly. Maybe we knew each other in another life, or our souls met before we were corporeal, I don't know how it works, but deep down it feels like I've known them for eternity. I felt it the moment I saw Mya, and now Madís. *Why the fuck did it have to be with a human?*

Mya sighs and puts her cleaning cloth and spray bottle on the counter. She slowly walks over and sits in the chair next to me. "Can I hold your hand?" I nod and she reaches over and takes my right hand in both of hers, "Do you want to try drinking from humans again?"

My stomach drops and I feel like I'm going to throw up, the tension in my voice starts to increase, "You know I can't Mya, you know that I hurt them every time, I can't, I can't, I can't."

"Shhhhhh, it's ok, I'm not forcing you to do anything, but we need to talk these things out, I can't let you just be in your head all the time. I know you prefer silence, but I also need to make sure I know how to support you." She pauses, letting me process everything that she's just said.

My heart is racing. Before I had the knowledge or means to acquire blood bags, I killed more than my fair share of humans when I fed directly. Getting caught in their memories made me unable to concentrate, so I'd either drain them or get too rough and come to as they lay in a crumpled heap on the ground. Their fate always depended on what they did to my system. Some are like a drug-once I taste their blood I can't stop myself even though I desperately wish I could. Certain humans' blood doesn't draw me in as much, but their memories do. Once I'm lost in their mind, I become unable to control my strength and I break their neck or crush their skull. The method in which I killed them didn't matter though, either way, I was taking something that I had no right to, and every time I murdered someone my guilt consumed me.

I made sure to only feed on people that deserved to die, but after a while even that wore on me. I became obsessed with researching people who would hurt others on purpose, and then I'd feed on them. I was the vampire equivalent to "Dexter." I caused so much death, so much destruction, it was pushing me towards the edge.

"I don't want to talk right now."

"I know it's really hard, do you want to get your device?"

I shake my head no, I don't want to express myself at all.

We both sit there, I'm staring at the table, she's looking at my hand as she still holds it. I realize she's right. I need to keep trying to work through this.

"I'm going to go get my headphones." She nods as I rush to my room. Grab my phone and headphones off my desk and rush back to the kitchen. I sit down next to her without looking at her. I put my headphones on and open my phone to my notes. I start to type at hyperspeed, my fingers a blur as I pour my thoughts out.

You know that when I was human, other people's energy had an overwhelming effect on me. We never figured out if it was because I'm autistic, because of my grandmother's gift, or a combination of both. People's energy radiated from their body like electricity, and I could both see and feel it. It's as if the air around them was heavy, it would buzz. Bad, happy, mad, it all sucked me in. In extremely disturbing situations it would hurt me for days, and I'd become unable to function because of someone else's pain. Remember having to nurse me back to health? Remember how hard it was for me to come back every time?

I had no idea that becoming a vamp would morph my ability and make it almost impossible to live. While I can still see people's energy, it doesn't bother me the way it once did; I'd kill to have that silly little bit of intuition be the only thing that I experience. Now, when I feed, I can feel everything that that human is currently feeling, as well as see their greatest fears, most painful memories, and proudest moments. Most vamps don't care about killing the humans they feed on, but I can't be let into a person's entire existence, and then be the one to extinguish it. I know I've said all of this to you a million times, but I need you to hear it again.

I hand the phone to Mya to read, these exchanges are easy because I'm able to type all of this in a matter of seconds and she's able to read it just as fast. She hands it back to me when she's done, and I begin to type once again.

You tried so hard to train me to feed without taking someone's life because you could see how much it hurt me, but no matter how hard you tried, the visions were too strong. I never learned to control myself while trapped in someone else's mind. When you taught me how to acquire blood bags it was such a huge relief. I really don't mind them; they remind me of drinking diet soda when I was human. Funny after taste, not as satisfying, but you get used to it after a while, and as long as I don't try the real thing it's not bad. I know I've told you all of this before, I know you've been through it with me, but I need to remind you why this freaks me out so much, why I can't go down that path again.

As I hand the phone to her I closely watch her as she reads my message. Over the years she learned everything she could about autism in order to support me as much as possible. Mya's fantastic at understanding what I need, and how to help. The night that I had met Madís in the club had been an exception, she'd been in a bad mood all day, and I was getting on her nerves. She tries hard not to tell me what to do but I'm sure that watching me connect with someone so deeply and then just walking away without tasting them killed her. It's the exact opposite of how she operates. She searches for humans that call to her, she derives immense pleasure when drinking from someone that arouses her heart just as much as her thirst. On the flip side I have no idea how she can do that, how she can feel so much at one time, hurt the person that is creating that bond, and then walk away. Then again, she doesn't kill them the way I do, so I'm sure that makes a big difference.

Sometimes we love each other like spouses and other times we fight like siblings, our relationship is so varied I've had a hard time explaining it to other vamps. They still think we're lying when we tell them we're not lovers. *Why is it so hard to believe that platonic love can be this deep?* As I'm thinking this I decide that I really do need a change of scenery.

Mya has put my phone down on the table by this point. She's studying the side of my face as I continue to trace the veins of the wood. "Thanks for the reminder V. You know I love and support you in everything, but I do have a really hard time imagining what you go through. I'm sorry if suggesting you feed was insensitive. Can I hug you?"

I think for a second, *do I want to be touched right now? Not really.* I shake my head no and Mya nods in acknowledgement, I can feel her love for me radiating from her warm glance.

She gets up from the table and goes back to cleaning the kitchen counter. As I sit there I think about how much she's helped me. I owe this entire life to her. If we hadn't met at *Evergreen* all those years ago where would I be now?

My heart has slowed to a normal pace, and the knot in my stomach is starting to loosen. I can feel my voice slowly returning. I look up at Mya and giggle as she's incredibly focused on removing a water spot, *She's so cute.*

"You're right, I need to get out of here. Let's go to that stupid party." I reluctantly say as I get up from the table, walk to the living room, and lay down on the couch.

She quickly looks up, surprise and excitement flooding her face. "Yesssssss!!! Oh my gosh, I'm so excited V! What can I do to get you ready?"

She runs over to the couch and kneels down next to me; she's fidgeting like a small child about to open their presents on Christmas. I can't help but laugh, she has such a beautiful smile, I could stare at it all day, at her...

Mya's nose crinkles and she gives me a mischievous look, "You know what this means? Barbie Time!" she squeals.

"No! Not Barbie time! I already said I'd go to your pretentious party!" I look at her with the most pathetic puppy dog eyes, knowing it won't make a difference. When we first met, my wardrobe was really embarrassing. Living off of a waitresses' salary in Los Angeles, I scrounged up whatever I could, and since I didn't care to get close to anyone, I wasn't looking to impress with my style anyway. Mya had a field day of course. We had our full on "Pretty Woman" shopping experience... I was in hell, but this super sexy, rich vamp was willing to save me from my sad little life, so I went with it.

"Come on! I know you secretly love Barbie time. Can I touch you?" I nod my head yes as I bite my bottom lip, I'm so turned on by her right now. She uses her fingertips to stroke my collar bones and works them down the center of my chest. Her icy fingers make me tingle with delight. I close my eyes and breathe deeply.

She goes over my black tank top and stops at my belly button and then works her way up. As I breathe, I'm almost purring. I open my eyes and turn to face her. Still acting annoyed I say, "You're such a brat, Barbie Time it is."

"Oh my gosh yes! I know exactly what to put you in!" Before I can even get up she's already bounding up the stairs at lightning speed.

As I trudge after her I remember how after a year of living with her I started to get my own style down, still expensive and posh but more vintage/goth. Mya was glad to see me finding myself and didn't mind that our styles were completely different. Since I am her little protégé she does have moments when she loves to dress me up, especially for vampire events.

She's a big deal in the L.A. vamp scene, and even though I couldn't care less about appearances, I know that it's necessary in order for her to keep her status. Even though I complain whenever she's going to dress me, she's right, I do like that I don't have to worry about it, and that she knows exactly how the other vamps will expect me to look. She has a section of her closet filled with clothes she has curated in my size, for occasions such as these. Over the years we playfully started calling it Barbie Time because it felt like she was a little girl dressing up her favorite Barbie whenever I gave in.

I'm slowly walking up our white staircase, knowing that it will take her a bit to set everything up. She likes a head-to-toe dress up, make-up and everything.

As I'm walking down the pristine modern hallway I look at the black and white pictures of her and I that line the walls, and I start to smile. I also have a second reason for enjoying this. I didn't grow up with any sisters, and my mom was too busy working to take me shopping, to show me how to do my make-up, or to teach me how to dress for different occasions. I also grew up in a traditional Mexican household where mothers didn't really do that, even if they had the time. My mom was there to put food on the table, a roof over my head, and to make sure that I went to school, not to be my best friend. I would watch TV shows and wonder if mother-daughter bonding time existed in real life, or if it was just something that occurred in make-believe families. The first time Mya took me shopping my heart remembered how I'd craved this as a kid. Nothing like a best friend helping to heal your inner child.

Chapter 7

As we walk into the multi-million-dollar apartment, "Chains" by **Al3jandro** is playing. Vamp bodies moving to music is something I'll never get used to. They don't make a sound, and they all move as if they're one. I've never been able to tap into this, and I feel like a turd in a punch bowl when I try-hence me wanting to dance with humans instead.

This apartment takes up the entire floor we're on. There are at least 400 vamps here, everyone dressed in the latest and most expensive designers. The Met Gala has nothing on vamps, they wear elaborate outfits multiple times a week and then throw them out like old rags, it's so wasteful! I remember just how much this environment bugs me and, as the champagne flows and the light flickers off of the crystal chandeliers, my skin itches to get out of here.

Suddenly, my pupils dilate, and I start to salivate, I can smell him. Even without my perfect memory, Madís' aroma is seared into me. *Shit! What the hell are you doing here Baby Boy?* I quickly scan the room because he's either been brought as someone's snack or is going to be claimed real quick. Sure enough I see them holding a tray of champagne, and they've already been cornered by the twins. Madís looks so adorable my heart skips a beat. They're wearing a white button-down shirt and black slacks. Their dark hair drapes over the right side of their face and hangs over their silver rimmed glasses. I wish I could bite those perfect heart shaped lips. *Ugh, get it together V, you need to get him out of here.* I take a deep breath and get ready to put on my Kardashian voice. I left him at that club so he'd be nowhere near this world, *Fuck!*

Whenever we come to these events I stand against the wall and people watch while Mya makes the rounds. She's already disappeared into the crowd knowing that I prefer not to interact. Madís has just changed the course of this night. I strut over and make pretend eye contact. As I come up to them I do the whole fake hug, kissy kissy thing.

"Bitches! Where have you been? It's been too long since we've chatted!" I exclaim.

Sandra answers, "You're one to talk! We're at all the parties and you're the one who's never there!"

As we're talking, I glance at Madís, who peers back at me with a raised eyebrow. They know this isn't the same person they met in the club. I showed them more of myself than I usually show people. I was happy and free with them while dancing, even though it was only for a moment. Here I must be rich vampire V, I need to act as fake and vapid as the company I, unfortunately, need to keep. My outfit isn't helping the situation either. Six-inch, diamond-encrusted heels peek out from under the hem of my long, copper-colored silk gown. While the plunging neckline reveals my natural lack of cleavage, the slinky fabric perfectly outlines my ample hips and booty. The color and texture of the material makes me feel naked, and I'm pretty sure that at first glance I look as if I'm wearing nothing. My make-up is also completely out of character. I tend to prefer a smokey eye with red lipstick. Tonight, it's a bronze natural look with neutral lipstick and an emphasis on my glowing complexion (that's what Mya said while she was doing my make-up anyway).

My mind wanders while the twins continue to chatter. It's hard enough for me to listen to any conversation for long, but vamp conversations are extra boring. People imagine vamp life to be sex, money, beauty, and death...and they're right. That's like literally all it is. Most think that's a dream come true, but when you take struggle, pain, and humanity from someone, what's left over is a vapid shell.

No amount of money can make these vamps interesting to me, and physical attraction can only go so far. Especially with my gift, a person's true beauty shows up quickly once I get to know them. The reason I'm so attracted to Mya is because her big bad vampire act is just that—an act. She puts on this invincible persona, but underneath her heart is so tender, it could be shattered at any moment. People have no idea. It's why she couldn't leave me in that restaurant all those years ago, and although most write her off as another pretty face, I know better. Even as my mind is elsewhere, I watch the twins' every move, until their facial expressions indicate that they've said something they think is super witty.

"Oh my gosh, that's soooo true!" I excitedly squeal. It's pretty cool talking to vamps while autistic. They're so self-absorbed I know I'm not missing anything, and they never notice I'm not listening. I just shake my head, throw in those *uh, huh, oh my gosh* statements and all is well.

As they're talking, I go into my memories and mull over why I'm so good at being what everyone expects me to be. When I was young it became apparent to all of the other kids that I was different. I loved to talk about my special interests to anyone who would listen, I'd stim openly, I had no filter, and processed emotions in my own way. The bullying started instantly; I was relentlessly teased for the way I acted, how I dressed, and the things I was into. I dealt with this for eight years; it wasn't until high school that I realized I had to change everything about me in order to fit in and avoid further harassment.

I would study my classmates as they talked, and watch shows and movies and mimic the way the cool kids acted. I would create scripts in my mind and practice them over and over again. I became so good at being who my peers wanted me to be that I lost myself in the process. While I was able to stop the scrutiny, that pain was replaced by extreme anxiety and depression as a result of suppressing everything I was meant to be. It wasn't until I was in my early 30s that I started to find myself again—my true autistic, queer self. I'm an expert at masking and transforming, but it does come at a price to my mental health. It's why I try to only do it in short stints.

They go on and on about their new yacht, the Italian villa they just purchased, how annoying their dad is. I continue to nod as I register enough info to comment, but I don't pay close attention to the details. Once they're done complaining about their father they pause in order to give me a chance to share what's going on with Mya and me. I can tell that they don't really care about me though, they just want the scoop on Mya, the most eligible vamp bachelorette.

As they've been speaking I come up with a plan for getting Madís away from them. If a vampire meets a human and wants to feed on them later they mark them with their scent to keep other vampires away. We release pheromones through our skin and saliva that leave a very distinct marker. If a vamp smells another vampire's scent on a human, proper vamp etiquette is to leave the human alone. Let's see how well I can spin this fairy tale.

"Oh my gosh I have such a random story to share with you two. So, Mya and I went dancing a few days ago and I claimed this waiter while we were there! When I saw you talking to him I was like, 'oh my gosh what are the chances!'" As much as I hate these parties, acting fake is really fun in moderation, and while I say this I'm frenemy-laughing, knowing that this piece of information is going to start a pissing war. I've spent my whole life pretending to be what others want. All of that made me the perfect vampire chameleon, and even though I do love the real me, "All the world's a stage" after all.

Britney responds with an exaggerated pout, "You're such a liar!"

"I marked him when I met him, feel free to check. I was planning on fetching him later tonight, and now he's here! I love it when things work out like that." As I say this I'm praying that I danced with him long enough to leave my scent. My skin did rub up against his plenty of times, so there's a good chance.

Madís has been standing there throughout this entire conversation. Since we were speaking about them-and the rich party goers were so interested in them-they wouldn't dare walk away from the twins. They've been standing perfectly still with a tray of champagne glasses filled to the brim. Britney is only standing about 5 steps away from him. She saunters up and inhales his neck deeply right below his chin. She is expecting to catch me in a lie, but once she rolls her eyes I can tell she's caught my scent. Just to annoy me she slowly traces his jaw from chin to ear with her tongue before she backs away.

"What the fuck?" Madís says under their breath, before quickly realizing their mistake; this stuck-up rich girl could easily cost them their job. Since they're unaware that their life is literally in danger, losing their income seems like the worst thing that can happen. I still remember working at the restaurant and feeling as if rich people had my life in their hands-one wrong move and they could crush my ability to survive. Madís shuts their mouth and just stands there, not knowing if they should stand up for themselves and lose their job, or just take being treated like an inanimate object.

"Whore! You did mark him! Oh my gosh, you have always been such a sneaky bitch. I always tell Sandra that it's the quiet ones we have to watch out for." Her hands are crossed in front of her chest and she's trying to hide how annoyed she is. "You win this time V, but next time there's no way I'm letting you walk off with our meal if you aren't here first." Britney tries to sound playful, but I can tell she's majorly pissed. Daddy's little princess isn't used to being bested, and although I'm glad I saved Madís from their clutches, I'm just as excited to have beat that smug trust fund baby at her own game.

I turn to Madís as the twins walk away. "Hi, angel. I need you to follow me," I say in my sexiest voice, every syllable dripping with lust. Aware that Sandra and Britney may still be listening, I have to control him with compulsion in order to keep up the ruse. He puts the tray down and follows me, completely in a trance. I walk him up to the roof knowing that we can be alone up there. The party's just started and no one will venture up here for a few more hours.

As we climb up the grey metal staircase I pull out my phone and text:

Anthony
Bring the car out front. I'll be there soon.

Once we're at the far edge I look him in the eyes and release him from my control. He jumps back, eyes wide, heavy breathing, "What the hell V?" When someone's being controlled by a vamp the release is jarring. Most people don't get released though, as they either end up dead, or are made to forget whatever just happened. On the rare occasions that a vamp does end the compulsion and returns a human to their normal state, that human's brain catches up with everything that's happened, and it's a huge jolt to their system. I try not to do it, but I had to get him out of there.

"I know this is all really weird. I promise you that I'm not going to hurt you." I hold my hands out as I say this, trying to make it clear that they shouldn't run.

"How am I supposed to trust you? I don't even know you! What were you guys talking about up there? Why did that woman smell and lick me? I know I don't have money but all of you need to stop acting as if you own those who work for you. Also, what did you just do to me?" I can see their mind racing, unable to get a sense of what just happened. Their light brown eyes shoot me a menacing look, even in the moonlight their olive skin glistens, and as serious as this all is I can't help but love how cute they look when they're angry. They run their right hand through their silky dark brown hair and draw their perfect pink lips in as they contemplate everything that has just happened.

I try to collect my thoughts, "All of this is going to sound ridiculous, but I need you to hear me out. You can't run, and you can't go back to that party. The me you met a few nights ago in the club, that's the real me. The person you saw down there is who I need to be to survive. Can you please stay with me long enough to listen?" They don't trust me, but they nod their head slowly. They're still staying a few feet away from me, but as long as they don't run, I don't mind.

"I'm going to be blunt and honest with you because it's how I prefer to communicate. You're at a vampire party. I don't mean people that dress up as vampires and drink fake blood; you're surrounded by actual blood-thirsty vampires." Madís shakes their head and looks down at the ground, the front of their hair falls over their right eye and they look up at me with an expression that says, *you've got to be kidding me.*

I don't let it stop me though, "The twins down there were ready to mark you as theirs. You wouldn't have lived through the night in their hands. I told them that I had marked you first, hoping that my scent would still be on your skin from when we danced. That's why Britney smelled you; she needed proof that you were already mine. Luckily, our interaction in the club lasted long enough for me to convince them that I was telling the truth. This really rubbed her the wrong way, as she's used to getting what she wants, so she licked you in order to try and get a reaction from me."

"Did it?"

"Did it what?" I snap back, annoyed.

"Did it bother you for her to lick me?" a devilish smile spreads across his lips.

"Are you seriously hitting on me right now? This isn't a joke, please take this situation more seriously." I roll my eyes and continue with my explanation, "I knew that since you were working, you'd be too worried about getting fired to come up to the roof with me by choice. So, I used vamp compulsion to get you up here. You're in so much danger right now. I need to get you out of here as soon as possible." I finish my explanation, and eagerly await their reaction.

They take a long, hard look at me, and then they start to laugh hysterically. "Who put you up to this? Was it Vincent? No, no it was Andres wasn't it? Wait, is Punk'd back on the air? Am I being Punk'd? Do I get to meet Ashton Kutcher?" They're practically falling over because of how much they're laughing.

I can't even begin to hide my frustration. "UUUUUUGH! Humans are sooooo annoying! This isn't a joke! There is a room full of hundreds of vampires down there! They will kill you if you go back down. Please, I really need you to listen to me," I frantically search my thoughts trying to figure out how to convince them.

Their tone quickly changes as they see that I'm not letting up, "I get it, you're some bored rich lady, who likes to mess with the help for fun. Go find yourself another server ma'am. I'm not a toy put here for your enjoyment. You may have Mexican roots but you're just as bad as them." He spits this last line out with so much disdain I totally get why he doesn't trust me. I really didn't want to resort to this, but I have no choice.

Chapter 8

I run up to him before he can even flinch, put my hands on either side of his angelic face and lick his bottom lip, it tastes so good I give it a tiny bite before I back away (I am a vamp after all), but I make sure not to draw blood. My eyes become completely black, my fangs emerge, and I look at him the way a wolf would watch a baby deer. I can hear his heart pounding, see the vein in his neck pulsing. It would be so easy to take a drink, *just one little drink*. I draw my head back and exhale as I bare my teeth; luckily, I've gotten used to controlling myself in these situations, and although it isn't easy, I know I won't hurt him. I come in contact with humans I want to feed off of all the time, so the act of self-restraint has become my specialty. It's like being in a restaurant with all of your favorite foods every single day, and not being able to have a single bite.

 I need him to see me, the real me...*all* of me. I need him to be scared and disgusted so that he gets the hell out of here, and never comes back.

He stands there staring at me, silent and motionless; I'm not even sure he blinks. I start to exhale, relief flooding over me. He's registering what I am, and he'll have no problem getting as far away from here, from me, as possible.

"Damn, you're beautiful..." he whispers.

I pull back, stunned. That's not the response he was supposed to have. *That's not how this was supposed to go.* My hands are shaking and my eyes become glossy. My lower lip is quivering as I try to explain how much of a monster I really am. "I'm designed to attract humans! Everything about me is meant to lure you, my prey. Trust me, I'm the farthest thing from beautiful." Looking at him is so painful, it takes everything in me to stay so close to them.

He looks deep into my eyes and with complete sincerity answers, "I don't think you're beautiful because you're made to attract me, I think you're beautiful because you could kill me in an instant, and I know you're not going to." They reach up and gently move my hair away from my right eye. "I was angry at you because I thought you and your friends were making fun of me, playing with me. I didn't think all that vampire shit was real, even after hearing you talk down there. I know I should be screaming my head off right now, trying to get away, but that's the last thing I want to do." They take a step towards me, they're so close I can feel their steady breath against my lips.

"That night in the club, when you looked into my eyes it was like nothing I've ever experienced before. I can't explain it, but it was like you were looking into my soul." They wipe their mouth and look down at the ground as if they're trying to recall something. "At first I brushed it off because I'd had a lot to drink, but even after that night I couldn't stop thinking about you. It's like you inserted yourself into my mind and a piece of you was left behind." As they say this last sentence, they reach out and touch my cheek with the back of their hand, before slowly moving their index finger down my face. My lips part in an involuntary moan, and the back of their finger strokes a fang before dragging it down to my lower lip. I slowly move my tongue out instinctually, and the taste of their humanity is almost more than I can handle.

Earlier I was so concerned with them listening to me I hadn't had time to enjoy the taste of their skin. I close my eyes and let myself truly feel their touch as the incredible warmth radiating from them draws my body closer to theirs. I'm not craving their blood anymore. I'm craving *them*. Every inch of them calls to me. It's as if we've been connected by an invisible wire that's pulling us closer and closer together. I want to be right up against them and never have to let go; I'm drawn to explore every inch of their body, and to make them groan with ecstasy as I do.

Suddenly, I'm jerked back to reality by the sound of steps making their way up the stairs. My vampire hearing is even better than the average vamp's because of my sensory processing disorder; I would have heard them way earlier if I hadn't been distracted by my desire. *No! It's way too early for anyone to make their way up here.* He notices the change in my demeanor and can tell something's wrong.

He looks around confused and asks, "What's the matter?"

"A group of vamps is coming up the stairs. They can't find you here. I need to get you out. Climb on my back," I order.

He scrunches his brow, "You showed me the fangs, the big eyes, I'm on board that vampires exist, but you look like you weigh 100 pounds and are like five feet tall; there's no way you're going to carry me."

"Are you fucking kidding me with this machismo bullshit right now? YOUR LIFE IS IN DANGER. I know what I'm doing and if you don't want your throat ripped out in a few minutes you will climb on my damn back!" I've totally lost my patience at this point; I'm going to freaking save his life whether he likes it or not. I'm all about consent but even if he doesn't give it I'm throwing them over my shoulder and getting the hell out of here.

My mom lecture helps him realize how much danger he's actually in, and that there's no time to argue right now. I turn around

70

and he climbs onto my back; I don't budge as he puts his arms around my neck and wraps his legs around my waist. Carrying him is like wearing one of those tiny little Fjallraven backpacks, and I don't strain whatsoever. I have to smile because I'm sure his bruised little ego is sulking right about now.

I turn and tell him, "Don't scream."

Before they can answer, I jump over the side of the building. I land without a sound, effortlessly, and don't even break my heel. I gently put them down and turn to face them. Their hair's a mess, their shirt is untucked, they lost their glasses, and they look like they've swallowed their tongue.

"I didn't want to give you time to think, the jump would have felt way worse with anticipation building." They don't say anything, and put their face in their hands while squatting down...oh no, are they going to throw up? Human fragility is probably the only thing I don't miss about being alive. "I get that you're having a moment right now but I need to get you home. Will you let me take you home?" They still don't answer, but they look up at me and quickly nod yes.

Lucky for Madis, my driver, Anthony, was in the parking garage and came as soon as I texted; I knew we'd have to get out of here fast and I didn't want to have to wait for a car. I hate driving, always have, so once I was rich beyond measure one of the first things I did was hire a driver- and buy a bad ass car, too.

This is a typical L.A. party so he drove me here and was then given access to the VIP parking garage below the high rise. By now he'd be parked at the front of the building waiting for me.

"Shit, Mya," I whisper under my breath. I open the slit in my dress and Madís' eyes look like they're going to pop out of their head as they follow the line of my leg up to my thigh.

"V, I don't think it's a good time to…"

I giggle and pull my phone out of my thigh holster. "Don't worry Baby Boy, I'm not trying to have sex with you while your life's on the line."

I quickly send a text to Mya. Knowing it won't seem strange since she's done this to me many times before.

Something came up, I'm taking the car. See you later. Love you.

As I'm doing that they turn around and exhale. I can hear them whisper to themselves, "I'm such an idiot, of course she wasn't hitting on me. Fuck this is such a screwed-up night." They still sound really confused, almost like they're in their own world, *I know that feeling well.*

Anthony is standing there waiting patiently for me. He quickly opens the door of my grey '53 Bentley and lets us both in. "Farewell and Goodnight" by **The Smashing Pumpkins** is playing as I push Madís in first, I have to guide them into the car as they seem to have lost the ability to recognize what's going on. "Madís…where…do…you…live?" I ask them as slowly as possible, but I am impatient since I want to get them home as quickly as I can.

"Koreatown" they answer while still in a daze, then they mumble the address. They are looking down at their hands as they wring them over and over again. A human wouldn't have been able to decipher what they were saying, but I catch it easily and relay our destination to Anthony. As we drive off, I roll down the window; the breeze feels nice and I'm hoping some cool air helps stabilize them. I turn to face Madís and see that they're looking out their own window. I don't need my vamp gift to imagine what they're thinking; I remember what it felt like to learn that monsters didn't just exist in nightmares, and to realize how close you were to losing your life to one. Then, to top it all off, I made the poor thing jump off a 20-story building. I put my hands on their shoulders and turn them to face me, before cupping their face and pressing my forehead up against theirs. They close their eyes and relax into my hands, then say, "You're so cold."

I smile and respond, "I'm your own personal ice pack." He opens his eyes and smiles. As he looks at me with complete innocence, I continue to cradle his face, "I know your whole world has just been turned upside down. If I could have kept you safe any other way I would have, but I couldn't risk just walking you out of there." As I'm speaking I move my index finger from the top of their jaw to their chin. Their breathing slows, it's calming them down. "It would have been too suspicious, and I'm too young of a vamp to pull crap like that. Everything seems really messed up right now, but you're going to go home, take a shower, and climb into bed. Tomorrow you'll still remember that vampires exist, and what you went through tonight, but it will be a hell of a lot easier to process."

His gorgeous almond-shaped eyes study me, trying to figure something out, "Are you controlling me again?" He still sounds groggy, as if he's awakened from a dream, but he's lucid enough to start piecing things together. He isn't upset, but I detect a tinge of fear in his voice.

My heart sinks. Even though he easily accepted that I'm a vampire, he knows what I'm capable of, and thinks I'd use it on him without hesitation, "I'm not controlling you Baby Boy, I've just been exactly where you are right now, and I know how it feels." I kiss him on the forehead and, just as I pull away, we park in front of his apartment complex. It's an older unit, built in the 90's and covered in bricks. The building is small, only two stories, probably 12 units in all. He gets out of the car, and I can tell that while he's still really shaken up, I can trust that he'll make it in safely. He turns around and looks at me with so much longing it takes all my strength to stay in the car. I can't get close to him; it would ruin him. *I would ruin him.*

For a moment I consider making him forget me. But knowing I'd never want someone to do that to me, I let him keep tonight. I let him keep the memory of me.

Chapter 9

The next night, I'm laying on my bed looking up at the ceiling, and listening to **The Smashing Pumpkins**, "Disarm" on my headphones; the music captures how I feel about Madís perfectly. The pain, longing, and frustration that I feel when I think about them melts into the rhythm and transports me, at least for a little while. Since I walk around with soundtracks in my head all the time I associate certain songs or artists with people, places, or feelings. Sometimes I listen on my headphones and sometimes I just replay them in my mind. I picture what the night could have been if I were human– bringing Madís home, making love with them, laying with them, and talking to them all night long. Instead, I'm alone, sulking and feeling sorry for myself.

My bedroom is the only thing in this house that doesn't fit the minimal modern theme. When I first moved in, Mya told me I could redecorate, so I ran wild. Money isn't an issue, she compels whoever she wants, whenever she wants, to get items or money. The entire house is modern construction, white surfaces, with wooden accents, but when you walk into my room you're transported into a cozy English den. The walls are a dark gray, there's a large fireplace on the far wall, and books line both sides of it. The vaulted ceilings are made of dark mahogany. My bed is round with a velvet emerald, green fabric headboard and base.

As I consider everything I rub the back of my palm up and down my headboard. I know I'm acting like a child but I get so tired of this life. I never felt like I fit in as a human, but I feel plain wrong as a vampire. When they existed in my fantasies it all seemed so effortless. It reminds me of social media. We love focusing on all the perfectly staged aspects of people's lives, but we don't take the time to acknowledge that nobody's life is flawless. Becoming a vampire made me acknowledge the ugly truth behind the façade, it forced me to look into the eyes of the man behind the curtain. We shouldn't be here; we're leeches that devour everything in our path. What good is eternal life when I'm living with this constant pain? With the inability to never truly connect with anyone. I know I have Mya, and I absolutely adore our relationship, but some days I want more.

I can spend days in my room thinking when I get into a slump. When I lay down, images run through my mind like a movie. I've learned to control most of them. If it's something I don't want to think about, I push it aside like I'm physically pushing a slide out of my mind. As I lay here, I don't try to control the images, though, I let the slideshow play unchecked.

I can't imagine myself in a relationship with a vamp, but I can't imagine myself with a human, either. Will I just be alone for eternity? I want to turn things off, to not feel so intensely, or care so much about how my actions affect others. Yet part of me loves this; because of these qualities, I find comfort in knowing that I won't become a soulless killer, addicted to the pain I cause. I know that my ability to love so deeply is an asset, not a weakness– but when everyone around you tells you that you're the one that's broken, that you're the one that's all wrong, it gets hard not to believe it.

People don't understand my train of thought, how I can jump from one subject to another, but this constant stream is always running through my head. I spend most of my life in my mind.

I start to wonder if my indigenous blood is in constant turmoil, fighting the urges of my vampire instincts. With my gift, I've often felt a deep connection to my Huichol ancestors, their link to this earth, and the bond they have with every living creature. I can feel the constant struggle between the part of me that is made to create, and the part of me that wants to destroy. I don't know if I'll ever be able to reconcile what lives within me, but I pray that I'm never taken over by the corruption that wants to flood my veins.

I look at the vines that crawl up my walls, that snake their way into every crevice, and I feel as trapped as they look. I thought being eternally bored was bad; now I'd take that boredom over this heartbreak any day. It's funny how when you're going through something, you think nothing else will ever compare to how bad things are—then something even worse happens and you look back and laugh at your old self. Silly me, sulking because I had to hang out with gorgeous, shallow vampires. Now I'm crying over a human and having an identity crisis... what's next?

Chapter 10

"Hmmmmmm... hmmmmmm... hmmmmm," I hum continuously as I alternate between hitting my palms together and tapping my thumb on each of my fingers over and over again, all while pacing back and forth. I stare at the dining room table; I've been avoiding looking there all day. The plain white envelope is sitting there; I haven't been able to control my anxiety since it arrived two days ago. It's ripped open and crumbled, the red seal bearing the Commission's insignia of a letter C wrapped in snakes is torn in half. As soon as I saw that stamp, I didn't need to open it to know what was inside, but my mind refused to believe that any of this was happening until I read the words.

My hands shook uncontrollably as I pulled the letter out and read the handwritten calligraphy. *Vamps are such saps for shit like handwritten, wax sealed letters,* I think to myself as I angrily unfold the paper.

Vampire V,

The Vampire Commission is summoning you for your required Service. We will call upon you in one week's time with the location you will report to, and the proper identification needed. Do not bring anything else with you, once you receive your information prepare to report the following day.

We thank you for your service,

High Council of the Vampire Commission

Stimming keeps me from throwing up, but it's not going to change that I've been called by The Commission. The Commission was created to enforce order in the vampire world. A squad of highly trained, highly skilled vampire soldiers working as one to make sure that no vamp ever gets out of line. *That isn't me...I don't know how to fight...I don't want to kill anymore...* The fear I kept brushing off as insignificant has finally come to bite me in the ass. I acted as if they wouldn't call me because the thought of me going was too terrifying to face.

"I can't do this; I can't do this..." my voice trembles as I talk to myself and finally it gets to the point where I can't hold it in any longer. I slump down to the floor and start heaving. I'm gagging but nothing comes out.

Mya runs out of her room, puts her arms around me, and rocks me back and forth. "Shhhh, shhhhhhh, shhhhhh, I know you're scared, just breathe, in through your nose, out through your mouth." As she says this, she strokes my hair. I focus on her voice, her gentle touch, and I try to breathe deeply. My breath follows her instructions, over and over again. I let myself go in her arms, and that's when the tears come.

Ten years, I'll have to serve them for TEN YEARS. That's the standard service time for anyone who is called to serve in The Commission. I never wanted this life. *I never asked to be turned into this.* On top of all of that, the little freedom I did have as a vamp will now be taken away. Working for The Commission isn't what scares me, it's what I have to do in order to be one of them. I'm going to have to drink blood from humans. I'm going to have to kill innocent people so that I can uphold this cruel society. I'm going to have to hide who I am after years of working to unmask. Up until now I couldn't stop them from killing humans, but at least I didn't participate in it.

Mya sits there holding me for hours, letting me cry, scream, and moan. She doesn't tell me everything is going to be okay, or that I'm overreacting; she knows how scared I am and she lets me process it all. An hour before the sun comes up, I've stopped crying but she's still rocking me back and forth, humming my favorite **Oh Wonder** song "White Blood."

"V, we need to go to our rooms, it's going to be light out soon. Do you want me to sleep with you today?"

I nod my head yes because the only thing keeping me together right now is her. We slowly walk to my room, her arm around my waist. I head straight for my bed and she clicks the button that activates the metal shutters. I lay under my weighted blanket in a fetal position and feel her slide in next to me. She drapes her right arm around me and pulls me in close. She gently kisses the back of my neck and whispers, "Whatever you need I'm here, I know I can't make things better, but I love you. I will always be here." I let out a scream filled with all the pain, anger, and frustration I've been holding onto for the last few days. I scream because I hate feeling out of control, I don't want them to turn me into more of a monster than I already am, and since I have to leave Mya, I'm worried my heart will break into a million pieces and I'll never recover.

She holds me as I scream, she buries her face in my neck, and I know she's just as scared that I won't make it back from this. *"Mi niña preciosa, todo pasará, y yo te esperaré aquí hasta que nos podamos reunir."*[10]

---

[10] My precious girl, everything will pass, and I will wait for you here until we can reunite; said in Spanish.

Chapter 11

As Anthony drives me to The Commission's training compound, "Angel" by **that dog.** plays through my headphones. It took us over five hours to get to the Sonoran Desert. I don't know exactly what part we're in as geography has always confused me, but it must be the section that's still in California because of the time it took to get here. I've been listening to the same playlist for the past two weeks. I haven't wanted to talk, eat, or interact. When I get really overwhelmed my instinct is to try and disappear, to go into my own world. I'll crawl into my bed with my headphones on and just lay or sleep for days. People used to take this as me being lazy, but my brain literally becomes unable to process any outside stimuli, I think of it as hibernating in order to let my mind catch up.

As we drive up to the compound, a large white concrete building towers over the desert landscape. It's jarring to see something so industrial right in the middle of the desert vegetation. The land rejects it, I can feel the way it disturbs the natural order.

I can't believe I'm going to have to live in this sterile place, that I won't be able to even talk to Mya for however long this training process takes. The song, "Angel", has been on repeat for an hour because it makes me think of her, and because it keeps me from crying for some reason. I can't walk into The Commission showing any weakness, I'll have to do without all of my supports, and I'll need to hide all of my autistic traits. After years of unmasking, I don't know if I'm going to be able to do this well enough to blend in. It's true that humans have a hard time dealing with people they don't understand, but vampires not only despise those who are different, they work to eradicate those differences—especially in a place like this. I don't want to lose myself. I don't want to kill for them. *I want to have control over how I live.* I spent my whole human existence living for others.

I was the oldest Latina daughter; my parents expected me to help raise my siblings and to often act as the go-to parent. As a female who was firstborn, I also took on the burdens of our entire family, the pain that my parents experienced, and the pressure to keep our family from falling apart. While feeling like an integral part of my family, I simultaneously felt like who I was was never enough for my parents. I couldn't come out to my family, couldn't openly love who I wanted, and was always misunderstood because of how my brain worked.

Once I became a vamp I was able to completely cut all ties. It was a coward's way out, but no matter how old I was I could never fully stand up to them. I never asked to be a vamp and I wasn't reveling in it, but I was living life on my terms, finally.

The car stops and Anthony opens the door for me. As I get out I can see that his eyes are glassy. He's worked for us almost as long as I've lived with Mya. Over the years we've grown to trust each other; he knows what we are and that we'll always take care of him and his loved ones. Once someone is with us for a few years we reveal that we're vampires and what that entails. It's really annoying to be sneaking around people that are always in your home, so finding reliable humans that we can trust is integral to our way of living.

He hugs me and says, "Once you're able to leave I will be right here, ready to take you home." I nod, take a deep breath and walk towards the compound that will be my prison. Since our lives are so long we are obligated to serve for at least a decade. Some vamps love it so much, they stay for centuries. I have nothing against the idea that we need this, it's just not for me. Vampires are too volatile to be left unchecked, and our society would crumble without The Commission. But as selfish as it is, I wish I could reap the benefits of its protection without having to participate.

I slowly walk up to a huge concrete building with no windows. It's ten stories high and the fence that surrounds the perimeter spans about two thousand miles. When you have endless amounts of money, building a top-notch training base is no problem. I scan the badge that was hand-delivered to me yesterday and walk through the double doors as if I own the place. From now on I will be flawless, I'm going to tuck my secrets away, pay my dues, and then get the fuck out of here. Luckily, it's easy for me to become whatever they want me to be, I just hope I don't lose myself in the process.

Before arriving here, I spent hours watching combat videos, army movies, reading everything I could get my hands on about The Commission. I know I can easily act like the cadet that The Commission expects me to be. The question is, what will it do to me?

They told me not to bring anything. I have the clothes on my back and nothing else. I don't care about my belongings, but I really miss my headphones, I feel like a body part is missing. The building is sterile and empty, gray floors, gray walls, and no unnecessary furniture or decor. It's been built to be an impenetrable fortress, a concrete box created to train killers. The lobby is silent and as I walk the squeak of my boots echoes because of the incredibly high ceilings. All that's in front of me is a four-foot-tall desk made of white marble. There's a vamp that looks like she's in her late twenties in human years. She wears a black fitted crew neck and sits typing at a computer. She's concentrating on the screen and doesn't stop to look my way. I walk up confidently and say, "Hello, my name is V, and I am reporting for my assignment today."

She still doesn't look up, but after a few clicks says, "You need to go to the third floor, when you get off the elevator turn left, then right and your orientation is in room 302." I stand there waiting for something more but she just continues typing. *Here we go.*

As I walk to the elevator all I see are gray doors, each with their own scanner for entry. Everything is lit by fluorescent light as there are no windows anywhere, not even on the doors (for obvious reasons). I step onto the elevator and realize that there are cameras every few feet. In the elevator there is a camera in every corner of this small 8x8 foot container. It feels weird to be so closely watched. Even though the hallways are empty I know that there is someone on the other side of that lens, scrutinizing my every move. They're already assessing me; as expected, my life stopped belonging to me the moment I stepped into this building. I take a deep breath, feeling claustrophobic at the thought of living like this for the next ten years. As a vampire in the outside world you get used to stares from humans, and criticism from vampires. None of it really matters, nobody was ever going to punish me unless I did something stupid and brought too much attention to myself among humans. Here, my entire future depends on if they like what they see, if I can be the perfect soldier for The Commission.

Once the elevator stops, I walk into a hallway that looks exactly like the one I just left. Following the directions I was given, I make it to room 302, scan my badge, hear a beep, and push the door open

Chapter 12

To my surprise, there is only one person in the room. He's sitting at a desk analyzing something on the monitor and the only other thing in the room is a single metal chair. I remind myself that, no matter how strange things feel, I need to command any situation I walk into. I confidently walk in and stand before his desk. I hold my hands behind my back, stand with my legs separated, look straight ahead, and say, "My name is V, and I was told to report to this room, Sir."

I can tell that his thoughts are in the middle of processing something. After a few seconds he looks up at me and says, "Please sit, cadet V." He has a stern look to him, but a gentle demeanor. He's Filipino, bald, with a thin frame, and dark skin. I'd say he was turned at forty-five. He wears the same crewneck that the woman in the lobby was wearing, with fitted black cargo pants, and combat boots. I do as he says and sit with perfect posture, hands at my sides, and eyes looking straight ahead.

"I see from your file that you are joining us from Los Angeles. You haven't been a vampire for very long, but we do tend to call the younger vamps since you're not as attached to your lifestyle as the seniors." As he's speaking, he's looking through a file of papers, I assume my entire life is printed on those sheets. "You are slated for the standard ten years of service, although you can be invited to serve longer if we feel you are a good fit here. You can also request an extension yourself. Your training will start tomorrow as soon as the sun sets." He stops reading for a second and quickly glances up at me then goes back to the paperwork. "You will be living on the seventh floor, room 715, where everything you need is already waiting for you. Our rooms are doubles; your roommate's name is Metztli, and they have been here for one year." Throughout this entire explanation his voice is monotone, and quick. He obviously wants to get me to my next destination as swiftly as possible. "We like to pair our new cadets with someone who has been training for a while. They will be your mentor and tutor for one year. Their official title is prefect. Do you have any questions?"

"No, Sir." I've been sitting there as still as possible, listening carefully to everything he has said, memorizing every detail. I will say that the emptiness of this room helps me focus, and I'm thankful for that.

"Very well, you are excused." He nods and then returns to his computer. I stand and walk out the door as if I know exactly where I'm going, and what I'm doing. I'm enjoying the directness and formality of this place—no need to chit chat, get right to the point, and then do what you need to do. Most people would have found that interaction cold and rude, but I liked it. Maybe I've been looking at this all wrong; maybe this place is exactly what I'd been looking for. Come to think of it, I've always lived in spaces that bombard my senses, everything in my life has always been so busy that I just accepted that that's how things have to be. Now that I'm in this minimal environment, with exact orders, and clear expectations, it feels like a weight has been lifted off me. I'm still terrified of feeding on someone directly, but at least blending in doesn't seem like it's going to be too hard. It's always good to have one less thing to worry about.

I get to my room, swipe my badge, and get ready to meet the person who may decide what the rest of my stay here will be like. As the door swings open, I'm met by one of the most beautiful people I have ever seen. They have long raven black hair that's tightly held in a braid, their face a mixture of indigenous and Middle Eastern features, with light brown skin, and beautiful big brown eyes. What strikes me the most are their lips—perfectly formed, wide set, and a dark pink color. As I take in their complete form my heart quickens; they're totally my type. Their large breasts are perfectly framed by what I'm assuming is the standard black shirt everyone wears here; their cargo pants hug their wide hips and perfectly round ass. I try not to exhale too deeply but I'm smitten.

From what I remember during my university studies, Metztli is a Nahuatl name, so they must be from Mexico. It's like I'm standing in front of an ancient warrior, a silent strength emanating from within. I forget my whole act and just stand there staring.

They walk forward with their hand extended. "Hello, I'm Metztli, my pronouns are they, them. We'll be roommates for the next year. After that I'll be put on assignment, and you will become a prefect." I shake their hand and, although they're not overtly friendly, I feel comfortable in their presence. Their energy flows from their handshake; it's warm and welcoming, and it betrays their cold outward demeanor. This place forces a formality on its Commissioners, but I can sense that there's so much more to my new roommate. *Shit! They're a soulmate, what the hell are the odds of meeting two of my soulmates in such a short period of time?* Maybe my gift's off, maybe I'm reading energy that isn't really there. Oh fuck, I need to listen.

Metztli starts to give me a tour of the room. Although not as empty as the office and corridors I'd been in, it's still very simple. Each of us has a bed on either side of the room. Next to each bed there's a nightstand, dresser, desk and chair. On my side of the room there's a door that leads to a simple bathroom where everything is white and spotless. They explain that we keep our room and bathroom neat and clean, as untidiness is not tolerated by The Commission. All of the clothing I will need is in my dresser.

There is a library in the compound if I'm a reader and would like to check out books, and I can also check out a device where I will be able to stream music. "They're strict here, but they also understand that they can't treat us like prisoners," they say with a smirk on their face. *There's the personality I've been looking for.* The whole time they're talking I just can't get over how gorgeous they are. I want to ask them personal questions, but I'm not sure if that's appropriate. Instead, I decide to keep up my "strong, silent type" routine. I'm known to overshare way too quickly, and this is not the kind of place where I want to make that mistake. I have an entire year to get to know them; I've got to pace myself, take my time, and keep my head down until I figure out who I can trust.

I've been nodding and listening this entire time. Once they're done talking, I just stand there awkwardly, not really knowing what to do next. They wait for me to say something, but once they realize nothing's coming they keep going. "We feed every other day. I hope you ate because our next feeding isn't until tomorrow." They pause to see if I'm going to react to this, when I don't they continue. "I don't know what you're used to at home, but it's a standardized process here."

The entire time Metztli is talking, I'm silently freaking out. *How am I ever going to be able to do this? I can act like a levelheaded, confident cadet all day, but once I feed there's no way I'm going to be able to block my connection to the human. Unless someone is standing there ready to yank me off them, I don't know if I'll be able to regain control.* My fingers start to twitch; I need to stim. Shit, I can't let them know how scared I am. In the most normal tone I can muster I ask, "Are we allowed to leave the building?"

"Oh yeah, there's a secure perimeter around us and we're also in the middle of the desert so there's no one for thousands of miles. You're allowed to walk around as long as you don't leave the fenced-in area. It's boring out there, though." With the way they answer I can tell they haven't noticed that my anxiety is building. They're probably assuming I'm just a nervous first timer.

I need to get out of here; I tell them, "I was stuck in the car for hours, and now being in here is making me kind of stir-crazy, I'm going to go take a walk. I like being outside."

They shrug. "Suit yourself, I'm going to head to the library, then chill in here for the rest of the night, so I'll see you later." I give them a strained awkward smile and start to head to the door. "Oh, I almost forgot. Curfew is at 0400, they don't want to risk anyone getting caught outside. Once 0500 hits, the whole building goes on lockdown."

I turn to them as they're talking and quickly nod to show my understanding. *I need to get the hell out of here.* "Sounds good, I'll see you in a bit."

Chapter 13

The moment I step outside, I take a deep breath. The cool desert air embraces me, bringing me back to earth. By the time I'd reached the bottom floor, I felt so anxious, I was worried I'd gag or start humming in front of the guard at the entrance. With the exception of Metzli, everyone here acts like I'm invisible, but I know they're watching my every move; something this organized can only exist with complete control. I can't let The Commission know how hard I am to regulate.

Even though I'm outside, I know that there's surveillance, so I still can't let my guard down. But the fresh air is already helping to clear my thoughts. I walk with my hands in my pockets and rub the nail of my thumb against the nail of my index finger over and over again. This was always my favorite stim in college, I enjoy the feeling and the sound, and because it was so easy to hide; for those same reasons, it's still one of my favorites. As I'm rubbing my nails together to calm myself down, I try to formulate a plan.

Tomorrow I'm going to have to feed. I'm going to have to drink blood from a live human. Is there anything that's ever kept me from getting lost in their thoughts? I think back to every single human I ever drank from; I remember each of them. Their faces, smell, and taste are burned into my memory.

MUSIC–the only other medium that is able to put me in a different headspace. I need a song that I can play in my mind, something that won't let me lose myself. When Mya tried to train me, her neurotypical brain didn't understand what I was going through. She tried helping me the way she would have instructed someone with her neurotype; no wonder we never figured it out.

Instead of being scared of my abilities I should have leaned into my supports. I run towards the building at lightning speed, scan my code, and walk up to the person at the desk. "Hello, I'm cadet V, where can I find the library?"

Without looking up from the computer, a young male vamp responds, second floor, room 230. I nod and head to the library as quickly as possible. I need to be back in my room in three hours and I want plenty of time to find what I'm looking for.

The doors to the library are double instead of single, but other than that it's the same gray, windowless entrance like all the other rooms in this place. I walk in after scanning my badge and am blown away by the enormity of the library. I know the compound's big, but my gosh, I would not have imagined something like this. This one room has three levels to it, and is about the size of a large performance theater. I don't understand architecture and how they make this fit within the floor plan but it's incredible. Beyond the library's sheer size, walking in here is like being transported somewhere else. This room is warm, full of color, it's nothing like anything I've seen in this compound so far, and the juxtaposition is so great I'm really thrown off.

Once I get over my initial shock, I notice a wooden desk to my right with an older looking Commissioner sitting there. He's reading a book and glances up as I walk towards him. He smiles and the warmth in his eyes reminds me of Mya; this is the longest I've ever been away from her in ten years, and my heart shudders at the reminder. I shake it off because, if I ever want to get back to her I need to get this figured out, and soon. "Hello, I'm cadet V, I just arrived. My prefect told me that I could check out a music device here."

He sits up excitedly. "Nice to meet you V, my name's Tomás. We haven't had a batch of new recruits in a while, good to have some fresh blood. I'd be happy to help you with that." He moves the mouse on his computer and then begins clicking and typing excitedly. There is so much energy coming off of him that I can see the air around him buzzing. As he looks at the screen he continues to talk and his pleasant demeanor makes me want to giggle, it's infectious. *What in the world? He's another soulmate!* There's something wrong with my gift. This place must be screwing with me. I have only met 3 of my soulmates in the 55 years I've been alive, and Mya is one of them. There's no way I've just met 3 more in the span of a few months. I can't trust my instincts right now; this can't be right.

I shake off my confusion and continue to listen, "You're going to be issued a Commission-sanctioned phone. You can't use it to contact anyone outside of the compound, but you can message people within the building if they have one also. It does not have a browser, but it does come with Spotify and a book app with unlimited titles in case you like reading digitally. Do you prefer earbuds or headphones?" He glances my way waiting for a response before he inputs it into the computer.

"Is it possible to get both?" I ask casually. I'm really trying to hide my excitement at getting to have headphones and earbuds, and the simultaneous confusion I'm feeling at having my instincts malfunctioning.

"No problem," he turns to a large bookshelf behind him that's lined with black boxes of different sizes. He pulls out a rectangular one, inputs the barcode number into the computer and then opens the box. It contains a simple black smartphone, a charger, black headphones, and earbuds.

I take everything and thank him. As I turn to walk out, I hear him quietly say, "V, I know everything seems overwhelming right now, but it's not that bad. Keep your head down, do as you're told, serve your time, and you'll be fine." I turn to look at him and tilt my head trying to figure him out. He crinkles his nose and winks at me.

What is that supposed to mean? Why did he feel the need to say that? Is it that obvious that I don't want to be here?

"Thanks for the advice, but I think I'll be okay," I say, while trying to hide the irritation I feel at this vamp possibly knowing more about me than I'd like him to. *Is my instinct correct, are we connected?*

He sighs and gives me one last look; I can tell he wants to say something else, but he decides against it, gives me a quick nod, and goes back to reading his book. As if this place didn't already hold a strangeness to it, this interaction has just added a whole new layer. I need to revisit this later, because there's something more to this vamp and space than meets the eye. Right now, however, I have enough to worry about.

I head straight to my bedroom, giddy at the thought of having something that I can use for comfort here, but I'm also focused on the fact that I need to find a song before the sun comes up. I walk into my room and look around, letting out a huge breath when I notice that Metztli isn't here. I get a trustworthy vibe from them, but I need to do this without having to explain myself, or feeling like someone may be watching me.

I sit on my bed cross legged and begin to search for a song. It needs to be something that can consume me, that I can fully focus on. I sit there scrolling through playlists, artists, and new releases. Nothing seems intense enough for what I need until it suddenly clicks. *Oh my gosh, why didn't I think of this before!* The title is a little on the nose but "Control" by **Halsey** is what I used when I was first turned. I've blocked out a lot of those memories, which is why I didn't think about it when I first started searching, but it's perfect.

When my hunger was insatiable, and I couldn't control myself as a new vamp I used to just keep this song on loop. The lyrics remind me of what I never want to become, and the melody puts me in a trance. I never thought to stim to music while feeding so I'm praying that this works—otherwise, there's no way I'll make it past tomorrow. I'm sure if I kill a human on my first day I won't be walking out of here alive. I've seen too much of this place, and without having the time to indoctrinate me, The Commission won't set me loose. I hear Metztli swipe their card, so I lay back in bed, making it look as if I'm relaxing as I listen to music. They walk in and notice that I have the phone and headphones. "I see you found the library—"

"There was a vamp at the desk, looking to be about 55 physically, white beard, short afro, do you know his story?" I interrupt without thinking, "Oh my gosh, I'm sorry you were in the middle of talking. When things pop into my head, I tend to interrupt people, I'm sorry."

One side of their lip turns up a little. "Don't worry about it, my little brother used to do that a lot, it's no big deal." They walk over to their bed and sit cross legged. "You're referring to Tomás, he's been the librarian here for like 400 years. He's an old vamp from Brazil; he's never given me his actual age but from events he's hinted at I've always guessed he's around 900." They're squinting and looking up at the ceiling, as if they're trying to picture Tomás at this moment. "Rumor is he's one of the deadliest Commissioners that ever served, and even though he was high up he craved something quieter. He requested to be allowed to serve as the librarian for the rest of his life. I've tried asking him about it, but he won't share." They shrug their shoulders, and slouch as they say this. I wonder if his refusal to open up to them hurt their feelings.

They quickly straighten up, "Wait, why do you ask?" They're starting to get more comfortable around me, and that makes me smile. The incredibly formal cadet that I met earlier that day is beginning to fade into the easy-going person I can sense is inside.

"When I went to check out my device, I could sense something from him." I bite my bottom lip and try hard to recall their energy. "I can't explain it yet, but I could tell there's a lot there." As I'm explaining I imagine his face, his dark eyes full of kindness, the energy he exuded. There was something else there that I can't quite grasp though, like a word that's on the tip of your tongue, but no matter how hard you try to recall it it's just beyond your grasp. I'm snapped out of my daydream by Metzli's voice.

"He's one of the coolest vamps I've ever met. I love talking books with him. He's smart and funny too. Take some time to get to know him before you make any judgements." Suddenly, Metzli shakes their head, "Wait, you felt something? Is that part of your vamp gift?" They ask excitedly and then quickly pull back with embarrassment, worried that they've crossed a line. "Sorry, I hope it's okay for me to ask that. If it's not, then no big deal. You don't have to answer."

I happily answer to relieve their apprehension. "We are going to be roommates, and I'm guessing mentoring means we're going to spend a lot of time together. If you're okay with it I don't mind sharing AND getting to know you better. I feel very comfortable with you." As soon as I say this a shy smile spreads across their face; they try to suppress it, but it's the smile of someone who hasn't connected with anyone in a long time.

I continue, "To answer your question—yes, and no. Before I was a vamp I had the ability to read people's energy. I've never looked too far into it but it definitely came from my grandmother and mother. Deeper than that, I don't know." As I say this I can picture the two matriarchs that helped shape my life. Their beautiful white hair, olive skin, and brown eyes. Faces full of soft wrinkles with wide smiles.

I push the images out of my head and continue. "Once I became a vampire I started to feel like I had that ability on steroids." I recount this memory and it still creates a strong pressure within my head. I rub the center of my forehead with my index and middle finger to try and relieve the pain, but I continue to explain. "I can read people through their eyes, smell, and blood. I also have a special effect on people; others tend to trust me without me having to do anything. I never have bad intentions or use it against them, but it does come in handy." By the end of my explanation the tension I felt while recalling my struggles has faded, and I'm once again looking towards Metzli, my brows furrowed. I never know how someone will react to my gift, and it doesn't always go well.

"Shit! No wonder! I'm going to be completely real with you and say that I've kind of been freaking out this entire time!" They throw their hands into the air and then place both of their palms on the top of their head, disbelief flooding their features. "I like serving in The Commission, but we get moved around so much I don't try to get attached to anyone, it will just make it harder in a year." They bring their hands down and gesture as they speak excitedly; "From the moment you walked in here I wanted to talk to you, get to know you, share things I've never shared with anyone! I thought maybe I was going soft." They look down at their knees as they shake their head slowly and then chuckle and look up at me, "Damn girl, I'm impressed!"

Now it's my turn to suppress a smile. I tend to not share the nature of that gift with others because I worry that they won't be able to trust me, or our friendship, once they're aware; never knowing what's a real feeling, or what my mind is doing to them. "The reason I'm sharing all of this with you is that I can see your heart, soul, spirit, whatever you want to call it." I open my hands wide to try and encompass the magic that makes them so special. "You're a badass, and you love just as hard as you fight." I sit very still and look deep into their eyes, letting their energy flood over me. "From the moment I saw you I knew I could trust you. I didn't want to freak you out though, so I waited until you seemed more comfortable with me to tell you." I look down at my hands, starting to feel a little embarrassed, realizing that waiting a few hours to reveal all of this isn't exactly taking it slow. "With some people it takes a few days, but your system warmed up to me really quickly." I look up hesitantly, "You're from Mexico, right? I've taken a lot of Chicane studies classes for fun, and I noticed your name is Nahuatl."

Their face is all smiles now. "I'm part Nahua! Nobody here has ever heard of Nahua, I'm like, come on! You live forever and you can't pick up some indigenous history books?" They've thrown their arms open to show their exaggerated annoyance and then bite their bottom lip while their beautiful dark pink lips form a gorgeous smile. "I'm sorry I can't stop smiling, this is so unlike me, I've never met a vamp like you before."

I giggle, "It's ok, I tend to hear that a lot."

I'm distracted by a low beeping sound and look around the room quickly, trying to figure out where it's coming from. It's like nails on a chalkboard for my senses so I shut my eyes, and plug my ears.

"V, are you ok? That's just our cue that it is time for bed."

I take a deep breath and slowly open my eyes, shit, I let them see my senses get overloaded. "Yeah, I'm fine. I have super vamp hearing, better than most. Stuff like that is hard to handle."

They creep to the edge of their bed and lean towards me. "The good news is you'll be able to use that to your advantage when we train, the bad news is you're going to have to get used to sounds like that."

"Don't worry, now that I'm aware of it it won't bother me as much. It's when I get caught off guard that it's hard to deal with." I straighten up and roll my neck, trying to shake my anxiety.

They're still looking at me as if they don't believe I'm okay, but they slowly start to talk again, "We'll sleep our usual 14 hours during the day and then when the sun sets the alarm will ring again. If there is ever an emergency the alarm will ring in the middle of the day." They pause to see if I want to say anything, I just nod and they continue. "Since there are no windows in the compound it's safe for us to get up and move. We'll just be a bit out of it since we didn't get our full rest." As they've been explaining all of this I've continued to nod, making sure to listen to every detail.

It's funny, all of the mannerisms that I do while talking or listening are for show. I could sit and listen to someone without moving a muscle, or showing any emotion, but by the time I was in high school I realized that that really freaks people out. It's easier as a vamp, but trying to listen to someone and perform my expected reactions is exhausting. I'm glad I can finally stop talking and turn in for the night.

"Sounds good. I guess it's time for bed." Having to mask while I've been here, and interacting with new people has taken its toll. My brain is ready to turn off and recharge. I change, brush my teeth, wash my face, and get under the covers. I'm really missing my weighted blanket right now; I can sleep without it, but I'll be restless at night. Before I close my eyes I say, "Metztli?"

"Yeah?" they answer drowsily.

"I'm glad you're my prefect. I feel safe with you." I had to tell them how much I appreciate them in case tomorrow doesn't go how I hope it will.

"Me too, V, me too," they say as they're drifting off.

Right before I fall asleep, random thoughts always pop into my head, it's comforting as my mind winds down from the day. Tonight, my thoughts are all on Metzli. I'm not sure how but vampires can sense each other's ages. You don't get an exact number, but you can tell if someone is brand new, super old, close to your age. I sense Metzli's not that much older than me, maybe around 70. Like the Commissioner said, they like to use young vamps. It makes sense that this works for them; the younger we are the easier we are to control. I hope they find me to be as cooperative as they expect. Unfortunately, a lot of it depends on tomorrow...

Chapter 14

Just as Metztli described, the alarm sounds at what I assume is 2000 hours, since that would be the expected amount of time for us to sleep. Even though I tend to get the most done when I first get up I always have a hard time actually waking up. I rub my eyes and slowly get out of bed, I change into the standard black top, black pants, and combat boots that are in my drawer (I'm so in love with this uniform). I head into the bathroom and wash up, then make sure my side of the room is tidy. Once I'm done I look to Metztli for further instructions. By this time I'm fully awake and ready for the night ahead. Noticing my eyes on them, they look up from the book they've been reading. They got up earlier than me, and waited for me once they were ready.

Before they speak they put their book on their desk and get up from their chair. I'm standing in front of my bed eagerly awaiting my instructions. "I hope you slept well, today is going to be a busy day. I'm going to go through my usual schedule and you'll shadow me."

They roll their eyes right before they continue speaking. "The older vamps get annoyed with new recruits, so they've set up this system. The newer ones like me do all the procedure training, and the experienced Commissioners focus on combat and strategy, pretty much turning you into the ultimate soldier." They take a rigid salute stance and act as if they're in front of a superior before shaking it off with laughter.

I'm so glad they're here, I'd be so nervous right now without them. They straighten up and gain their composure. "You're going to shadow me for three days and then you will have the same schedule as me, but you will be in a group of new cadets. Your training will start off as basic, and then it gets harder as you learn more." They start to walk to the door, and I follow behind them. As they reach for the doorknob they pause and turn around, "Oh shoot, I forgot that today is a feeding day, so the schedule's a little different than tomorrow's. At 0200 we will be dismissed to our rooms for half an hour, which gives us a chance to clean up after a long day of training. Then at 0230 we report to the basement, level 1A." They say all of this as an afterthought, assuming that talking about feeding is as normal to me as would be expected from any vamp.

I gulp and try to keep my breathing even; my fingers start to twitch and it's taking everything in me not to stim with my hands.

Their eyes quickly dart to my fingers, they notice the twitching and stop talking. They look up at me, a questioning expression on their face and they slowly continue with their explanation. "We each get our own donor—which, by the way, is The Commission's official term, but different vamps call them different things." I've balled my hands into fists at this point but I notice that their eyes keep scanning my body as they speak. "Frankly, some terms are pretty disgusting, considering that these are human beings; but I'm sure you know that there's no point in trying to force compassion onto imbeciles." They say this last line while looking deep into my eyes. People don't usually notice my small twitches so quickly. *Shit! I should have been more careful.*

I work to make my voice sound casual and even. "Ignorant people bug the hell out of me."

They nod but are still searching my eyes, trying to figure out what my deal is. We've been face to face this entire time and I just keep focusing on their hairline, trying to act as neurotypical as possible. They continue their explanation because I can tell they don't know what else to do. "The donors have a device on their wrist that monitors their heart rate, blood pressure, and the amount of blood that is being taken. Most of us are able to feed for five minutes before the monitor starts to beep. When you hear your monitor beep you stop drinking, step away from the donor, and their guard will walk them out."

I'm listening to the feeding instructions with a huge lump in my throat. I just need to stick to the plan and hope that it works the way I think it will. I finally drop my act and ask hesitantly, "What happens to the humans once they leave?"

They deeply exhale, rub their eyes, and their tone softens as they answer, "V, I'm more than happy to answer that later today, but we do have to get going. One thing I have to say is, if you're a human sympathizer you can't let anyone know."

My eyes widen and I feel like I want to throw up, "Metzli..."

They quickly cut me off. "You were right when you said you could trust me yesterday. I now know I can trust you too..." They smile and get caught up in a memory, "I actually had a really cool dream about that." They shake their head and focus again, "but I'll also have to fill you in on that later. I will do whatever I can to teach and protect you while you're here, but you need to make sure you do everything exactly as I instruct you to." They've put their hands on my shoulders and are scanning my eyes, their face is just a few inches from mine. They want to make sure I understand how serious their warning is.

I answer with a tone that is just as serious as theirs. "I understand. Don't worry about me, I can do exactly as you say." Without warning they reach up and slowly stroke my cheek with their thumb. I inhale deeply and I feel butterflies in my stomach.

They quickly back away. "I'm so sorry I did that; I don't know what came over me." They're looking at the ground and they back up until their back is against their desk chair.

"Metzli it's ok, you took me by surprise, but you have nothing to apologize for." I take two steps forward and then pause to gauge their reaction. They're still looking at the ground but they don't try to move away from me. I slowly walk up and place my index finger under their chin. I lift their face up to look at me and notice that their eyes are glossy.

"Metzli, are you okay?" They nod but don't say anything. I look deep into their eyes and so much pain is emanating from them that it's hard for me to be so close, *it really hurts*. "Is there anything I can do to help?" They shake their head no. "You don't need to speak, when you're ready, lead me out."

They close their eyes and take a deep breath, exhaling deeply. When they open their eyes they walk around me and head to the door. I wish I could do more to help, but whenever they're ready I'll be here.

I need to clear my mind now. I straighten my back, lift my chin, and take a deep breath. My head's spinning but I need to be the most obedient cadet The Commission has ever seen, and I can't let anything get in the way of that, not even Metzli.

Chapter 15

We make our way to the tenth floor and walk into a huge training room. It's separated into stations. My eyes are immediately drawn to the weapons section. I haven't had any previous training in weapons fighting, but I've always wanted to try to learn how to use them. The wall is lined with fighting sticks, swords, knives—anything you can imagine for hand-to-hand combat. There is a large mat in the center, as well as numerous smaller mats around the room.

There's another area separated by plexiglass that I think is for virtual simulations, based on the headsets I see hooked onto the wall. There's a rectangular area tucked into one of the walls, separated from the main room with a large window; from the ten chairs lined up beyond the glass, it looks like a viewing station. I shudder at yet another reminder that They are constantly watching.

While I've been taking it all in, more cadets and their prefects have lined up. Our group consists of about twenty pairs, all standing at attention against the wall farthest from the weapons. There's just enough space for us to line up shoulder to shoulder. I use my peripherals to look down the row but everyone looks identical. We're all wearing the standard uniform, and when I don't know someone well it's very hard for me to recognize the difference in people's faces. I'm really going to have to work on my ability to tell people apart here.

I also keep thinking about how this whole operation is genius; vampires make the best soldiers. We could stand here all day, our muscles won't get sore, and we won't get tired. We could even put ourselves into a sort of trance to keep our minds busy; we still need to be fully aware of our surroundings at all times, but if we have to stand in one spot for long, it makes the time pass very quickly.

From what I've read before coming here we'll train in this facility and once we are ready, we'll be deployed to serve in units around the world. Humans notice so little it's almost amusing, but since The Commission's creation hundreds of years ago the Commission units are in charge of keeping order in the vamp world, and apprehending any rogue vampires that refuse to comply. If a vampire or group of vampires becomes too powerful, reckless, and attracts too much attention in the human world we're dispatched and tasked with bringing said vampires to The Council. I'm pretty sure we're never supposed to kill our targets as The Council is hell bent on reprimanding the offenders themselves. My research didn't uncover what happens to vampires after they are turned over, but I sure as hell wouldn't want to be in a situation where I'd attract The High Council's attention.

My train of thought is interrupted when the door to the training center opens to the most commanding woman I have ever seen. She's about 5'10", has brown shoulder length hair, and is built like an absolute powerhouse. Once we're turned, our bodies will never change again, so she must have been a professional lifter, shot putter, or some other kind of major athlete in her human life. Her frame screams strength, and although she is muscular there is also a softness to her body that is quite beautiful.

She stands in the middle of the line facing us. Her voice is cool and clipped. "Goodnight, cadets. I am Lieutenant Marshall. You will stay here at attention the entire day. You will watch your prefect train. We need complete silence and no distractions. If you have questions, save them for the end of the night when you will be debriefing with your prefect. Prefects, find your name on the screen and report to your station."

A wall-mounted video screen that's on the right side of the room about twenty feet away turns on, displaying three columns labeled Station 1, 2, and 3, each followed by a list of names. The vamps don't need to walk up to the screen, they can easily read it from where we're standing; they all move to their stations without hesitation. I notice Metztli under Station 2, they walk to the one with all the mats, which are each about 10x10 feet. Even though I'm across the room from them I can hear their Gunny going over today's training session. "We'll be reviewing and practicing Krav Maga. I'll assign you to your sparring partner, as soon as you're matched up choose a mat."

Metztli gets paired up with this huge prefect, who towers over them at 6' 5" and looks like he must have been a linebacker when he was human. Metztli is fierce but I have to admit I feel nervous for them.

Since the prefects have been training for a year they know exactly what to do. Each pair converses for a moment, bows and then starts sparring. They're both good but I soon realize that I've underestimated Metztli; not only do they move with incredible grace but they're able to use their opponent's size and strength against him. It's amazing to watch, both for the combat techniques on display, and for the obvious mutual respect between the fighters. Despite each attack and counterattack executed with fierce precision, there's no malice or anger in the fight. When one beats the other after each round, they discuss what went wrong and come up with solutions for how to approach a similar situation. It's all very collaborative and amicable; I'm impressed.

This goes on for six hours, no breaks. Metzli practices with their partner the entire time. Sometimes they're sparring, other times they're practicing technique while offering constructive criticism on how to improve. Their instructor stops at each pair for about two hours to observe, provide feedback, and answer questions.

The cadets remain in our places, still except for our eyes following the action at each station. Neither the vamps sparring, nor those of us observing show any signs of physical or mental fatigue, despite the long duration. I'm mesmerized by Metzli, so I watch them the entire time. I'm going to be observing for three days so I'll get a chance to focus on the other stations then. At 0300 Lieutenant Marshall—who's been walking around, giving orders, and speaking with each section trainer—calls the prefects to line up in front of us.

"Prefects, today is your cadet's first feeding with us. Every vampire has their own feeding ritual, and our rules may be difficult for them to follow at first. Take them back to your rooms to prepare, and then report to floor 1A at 0230. You are dismissed."

Each prefect files out of the room in a single line before the cadets follow in the same manner. When we enter the hall, our prefects are waiting for us, and although nobody's talking, the atmosphere does feel more relaxed than when we were in the training facility. The silence continues as Metztli and I walk to our room. I'm still processing everything I just saw and don't want to talk yet. When we finally arrive, I turn my desk chair around to face Metztli's bed, where they sit cross legged with their back against the headboard.

"What did you think, V? Questions? Comments?" They're excited and are genuinely interested in hearing what I have to say. They sit and wait patiently as I continue to go over the whole day in my head.

"Honestly, that was AMAZING! You're like the ultimate warrior on the floor. I was nervous when I saw how big that other vamp was. It really surprised me how respectful and synergetic the training is." I'm excitedly talking with my hands as I continue, "I've always heard stories of how ruthless The Commission is, so I really didn't expect for the vamps here to act like this." The entire time I'm talking, I continue to go through my memories of the training. Since I don't like to look at people, I tend to think of other things while I'm interacting. It also helps me to remember what I want to ask.

"Oh yea, Tim is super cool—really intimidating because people still make assumptions based on looks, but he really is a stand-up guy. Martial arts have always been a passion of mine, so I did have lots of training before I came here. When I turned my gift manifested physically. My fighting skills are next level and I'm more agile than your average vamp. We all have our special talents though. As we train you'll work to see how your gifts can be used at your advantage." Metzli is nonchalantly cleaning their left fingernails with their right thumb as they say this. Cleanliness seems to be a big thing with them.

"I know what you mean about fearing The Commission; they're really the only thing that can stop a vampire. To be immortal, yet to know that there's an entity out there that can kill you in an instant, starts to create a lot of fear and distrust towards that institution. Once you get here you understand that The Commission is interested in order, not torture." As they explain this it's almost as if they're reciting a script, it sounds unnatural and rehearsed. "They teach us that we're only as strong as our weakest link. When we go out on missions we have to work together because we have no idea what kind of vamp we're going after." I continue to study them as they talk, *is this what they really think or what they've been forced to think?* "I've heard stories of some wicked killer vamps they've had to take down. It's in our best interest to work together, and to support each other so that we're stronger as a group. There's no room for egos." As I'm listening I'm really surprised at how committed to The Commission Metzli is. From their energy, the ties to their ancestral lands and people, I really wouldn't think they'd be so in tune with an association like this. *Such a strange contradiction.*

I'm still closely listening and nodding as they continue their explanation, "I'm sure you noticed the observation room. Every week, The Council that's in charge of running this Commission Training Center comes to watch us. They pay attention to each cadet and prefect, looking for warning signs of someone becoming too aggressive, unable to work with the group, or any red flags signifying that they're not going to protect their team the same way they'd protect themselves." This last line hits a nerve, and I twitch slightly. At this point they've laid back in their bed, hands behind their head and they're looking up at our white ceiling. They don't move their eyes towards me or try to sit up so I don't think they've noticed how hard this is for me to take in. *I really hope a lifetime of pretending has made me good enough to do this.*

"If The Council notices anything concerning, the vamp in question is pulled out right away. The cadets and prefects don't know what happens to those vamps, but we never see them again," their face was cool and collected the entire time they spoke but as they relay the last bit of information the tone of their voice changes, as if a memory has begun to play in their mind, and they're no longer in this room with me. I am well versed in losing yourself to your thoughts, so I can spot it very quickly in others.

Despite the bond we've begun to develop I don't probe to see if Metzli is speaking from personal experience. They'll tell me if, and when, they're ready. As they're lost in their thoughts I gulp. This was my biggest fear. What if I can't fall in line the way They want me to? I don't foresee myself being flagged for aggression, but I have had a hard time fitting in with vamps before, which might label me as someone who's not a team player. I'm good at becoming what others want me to be, but I don't know how skilled this group is at noticing when someone is hiding something. I'll just have to worry about that when the time comes because I realize that we've been talking for longer than I had planned, and I haven't started preparing for tonight's feeding. My eyes get huge and Metztli notices. "You, okay?" they ask, worry clouding their features.

I had been rehearsing my excuse for zoning out before feeding, "Oh shit! I just realized I haven't started my feeding ritual. I always listen to music before I feed, it gets me in the mood." As I say this they shake their head to show understanding, it's actually pretty common for vamps to have feeding rituals. Some vamps wet their appetite through violence, others through sex. Some rituals can be a little on the OCD side, but merely having a feeding ritual isn't unusual.

They answer, "No problem, I'm going to take a shower, that's part of my ritual, and you do you." As they're collecting their fresh clothes, I take out my device and start listening to "Control." My plan is to listen to the song over and over until we need to leave. One of the supports I created for myself when I was younger was listening to a song again and again. Then, when I'd have to take my headphones off (like if I had to go to school, or any other space where it wasn't allowed), I'd still be able to continue playing the song in my thoughts, even though I'd unplugged. There were times where I would forget that the song wasn't playing anymore because it was so vivid in my mind. This became one of my favorite coping mechanisms.

I'm hoping that when I play the song in my head it will be a strong enough distraction to let me feed without losing control. I listen to the song the whole time Metztli gets ready. Once they're done they say, "Did you have any more questions about feeding?"

I have my headphones on but I can hear them perfectly. I slide them off my head and rest them around my neck so that I won't be distracted while I think. I replay the memory of our conversation and answer, "No, you're really clear in your explanations and I appreciate that, it all seems pretty straightforward."

"Let's go then, I like to be early. I feel calmer knowing there won't be any delays or surprises," they stand and wait for me to put my device in my nightstand. As soon as I'm ready they walk to the door.

We make our way to the first floor of the basement without talking. I really like that Metztli doesn't feel the need to fill silence with small talk and chit chat. Part of it is the shared lineage but there's an understanding between us, like we could just sit together in silence and be content. I know I've been doubting the fact that my senses are telling me that Mádis, Metzli, and Tomás are all soulmates but my connection to them really is all consuming, *there's no way I'm making this up.* I'm happy just being near them and feeling their energy, and I can tell they feel the same about me.

Chapter 16

We walk into a concrete room, empty except for the five pairs of Commissioners in training already standing in line at attention. We file in as the sixth pair. I stand there waiting for everyone else to arrive and for feeding time. Once in position, I retreat into my own world; physically, my posture is perfectly straight and my eyes are trained forward, but I'm able to let my mind wander. I think of Mya, our home in L.A., what it will be like when I get to leave here and be with her again. Her memory gives me so much hope, and also reminds me why I need to be in full control.

I'm awakened from my daydream by a loud beep. I use my peripheral vision to see that all forty of us are here, lined-up, as unmoving as statues. The door clicks open, and an officer leads a single file line of humans in. My face remains stoic, but I feel my heart break. The "donors" have been compelled and are in a trance. They're wearing white scrubs with wide necks for easy access, their eyes are glazed over and bloodshot, they look gaunt, pale. When we get back to our room I need to ask Metztli more about this.

The humans continue to walk single file until each one is paired with their own vamp. The officer is barking commands the entire time. "Donors stop!"

Each humans' shoulder has stopped at their vampires chest, making a T shape. I force myself to breathe steadily, trying to hide my nervousness. My designated human is 5'5", with light brown hair tied back into a low ponytail that ends halfway down her back. She looks straight ahead without moving, and I can see numerous scars around her neck. My hands are shaking, *there's something wrong with her smell.* The best way to describe it is that she smells stale, my stomach turns, and I take deep breaths to stop myself from gagging.

Her monitor is on her right wrist, a black band with a small square screen in the middle. I hear the officer say, "cadets and prefects, step towards your donor. At the sound of the beep, start to feed."

I start playing the **Halsey** song in my head and I take a step forward. As I prepare for our connection, I think about how vampires can control their victims while they're feeding; it's an intimate experience and, while our fluids mix, we're able to create a psychic connection to direct that human's feelings and thoughts for the duration of the feed. Some vamps are better at it than others, and my gift allows me extra advantages when I do this. Other vampires prefer for their victims to feel pain, to be in agony. They get a rise out of it; I've never understood that kind of cruelty.

If I want to, I can transport my victim's mind somewhere else. The problem is, I'm usually so caught up in their thoughts I can't stay clear-headed enough to manage my power that well.

Beep! Beep! Beep! Here goes nothing. I tilt my head to the left, and quickly sink my fangs into her soft pink flesh. I can't keep my eyes from rolling into my head. I haven't fed from a human in ten years and the temperature and taste consumes me.

It's so warm and the metallic taste feels like liquid gold flowing down my throat. As I suck, I lick her skin, getting a taste of the saltiness that covers her pores. *Why have I kept myself from this for so long?* All of a sudden images start to flash through my mind, a newborn baby on my chest "She's beautiful, oh my gosh" ...a screaming match in a messy kitchen "Get the fuck out Jack, get out!"...an elementary awards assembly "Woooo, good job Andrew!"... *I want more, I need more.*

Suddenly, an image of Mya pops into my head. She's resting her back on my velvet headboard at home and I'm leaning against her chest. She runs her fingers through my hair as she kisses my temple and then my ear. She whispers, "Can we please stay here forever?"

I look up at her with a huge smile and answer, "Of course, my queen." Then rest my head against her chest again.

I'm snapped back to reality, and I remember that I need to use everything within me to restrict my hunger. I focus on the song, playing it over and over, turning up the volume in my mind. I imagine myself when I used to lose control, covered in blood, eyes that were unrecognizable, having lost all sense of reality.

While I can still feel the delectable liquid passing my lips and coating the inside of my mouth, I am able to disconnect. I'm able to put a wall up to block her memories, feelings, and essence from entering my mind. With this newfound clarity, I start to push every enjoyable moment I can recall into her mind. I fill her with joy, calmness, and safety. Her body relaxes, and her breathing smooths as if she's in a deep, comfortable sleep. *Beep! Beep! Beep!* I gently pull my head back, take a step away from her, and return to my formal stance.

I did it, I actually did it. My face masks the relief and pride I feel both at facing my fear and unlocking another layer of my powers.

The officer walks the humans out and, as soon as the last one reaches the door, the first prefect follows to lead our line out as well. Once we're out of the room we walk up the stairs single file, heading to our rooms for the night.

As soon as the door closes behind me, the words tumble out of my mouth. "I need to know what they do to the humans. Please don't tell anyone I'm a sympathizer, but I need to know."

Metztli lowers themselves into their chair slowly, their energy is detached. "They live underneath the first floor of the basement, floor 1B. They're kept in cells most of the day and are always under compulsion. A guard takes them outside and walks them a few hours a day; they're fed three square meals." As they describe this horrendous system their voice and face is devoid of emotion. "They have different units of donors so that we're only feeding from a unit once a week. They try to make a group last at least three months. Usually, after three months, they die. I don't know if it's the constant feeding, the captivity, or the twenty-four-hour compulsion, but their minds and bodies just give out. Those that don't die are exterminated." They pause for a second as their voice quivered a bit when they said that last line.

"A few weeks before a unit reaches its three-month mark, They start collecting a new batch of humans. They'll post a fake job ad online, something that's too good to be true, for desperate people trying to get by." Their face sneers in disgust and their eyes aren't focused on me, they're clouded over and vacant. "There's a strict vetting process in order to figure out if anyone will miss the person once they're gone; if it's someone who can disappear without questions being asked, then They store them until there are enough to make a unit. They ship the new group over after They take care of the leftover donors that haven't expired yet." Metzli's eyes regain clarity as they turn to look at me. Their long black lashes almost brush their eyelids as their black pupils bore into me.

I'm stunned, silent, and my eyes sting as I force my tears back. I know that human lives mean nothing to vampires, but how can They treat them like that? *We* used to be humans! How can They forget that so easily? There are thousands of vampires around the world that kill humans for nourishment and for fun, but until this moment, I was always able to ignore that horrible truth; I was able to live in my little bubble, drinking my blood bags and staying content in my ignorance. Now, the truth is not only staring me right in the face, I'm partaking in it.

I start to dry heave and run to the bathroom. I have a belly full of blood and it's plausible that I'm going to throw it all up.

Metzli runs up behind me and starts to rub my back. "V, I'm here if you need me."

I take deep breaths as tears stream down my face, I force the dark liquid down as it keeps trying to make its way back up. I start to rock back and forth. "It wasn't supposed to be like this, I'm not supposed to hurt anyone, I didn't want to be like this, please wake up, please wake up, please wake up..." My fists are clenched and I'm digging my nails into my palms. I can feel them ripping into my flesh and I welcome the pain.

Metzli quickly leaves my side and all of a sudden, I feel my headphones getting placed onto my ears. I can hear them scrolling through the phone and then the familiar melody of "Why Am I Like This?" by **Orla Gartland** floods my ears. I close my eyes and continue to take deep breaths. "Put it on loop," I mutter. They nod and press on the screen.

I scoot away from the toilet and lean my back against the glass shower door. I pull my knees up to my chest and, with my eyes still closed, tuck my head into my chest. I quietly hum to the music as I hug myself as tightly as possible. Metzli kneels next to me the entire time without moving.

The curfew bell rings, and I slowly look up at them. Suddenly I'm no longer thinking about the humans and a new fear consumes me, my hands start to shake, and I can't speak. I just had a meltdown in front of Metzli, *FUCK!*

I open my mouth, but words refuse to come, I honestly don't know what I'd say even if I could speak right now.

Metzli warmly smiles and says, "You're autistic, aren't you?"

I gasp and tears fill my eyes, but I still can't respond. "You have no idea how safe you are with me. My little brother's autistic, he was my best friend when I was human."

They're still holding my phone, so I reach out and gently take it from their hand. I open the notepad and start to type:

I'm sorry you had to see that

Then show them the screen. They read the message and answer, "You never have to apologize to me for who you are. Can I help you get ready for bed?" I nod yes. They gently hold onto my elbow and help me sit up, I feel dizzy and the warm strength flowing from their hands helps to calm me. They walk me over to my bed and I sit on the edge.

Metzli pulls my boots off, unbuttons and pulls my pants off, and carefully puts them away in the hamper. They walk over to me and take my hand in theirs. With extreme tenderness they walk me to the side of my bed. I crawl in and they pull the covers up to my chin. They sit on the floor right next to me and as they look into my eyes they run their fingers through my hair, I close my eyes and sigh. With my eyes closed I picture Metzli standing in front of me.

Their gorgeous broad shoulders are complemented by an exquisite long neck, and the curve of their waist as it feeds into voluptuous hips and ample thighs is not just beautiful, it's the strength and power of our earth. I can simultaneously feel the extreme compassion that lives within them, their body is a dichotomy of destruction and creation.

I open my eyes and they're still staring at me, concern strewn throughout their beautiful indigenous features. They stop stroking my hair and they begin to undo their long black braid; their expression turns more serious as they begin to speak. "I told you earlier that I needed to talk to you about a dream I had, but things have been so busy I hadn't had the chance. Yesterday, when I slept, my *Abuela*[11] came to me in a dream. She told me that I could trust you, and that I needed to help you. She gave me a *cempasúchitl*[12] and then disappeared. Whenever I need my ancestors' guidance, they appear to me while I sleep. Us meeting was not a coincidence or luck; our friendship is meant to be." By this last line their hair is fully undone and is laying like two dark waterfalls over their shoulders. They even contain ripples from the fact that they're always kept in a braid. It takes everything within me not to reach out and touch their hair, it's so mesmerizing, it feels as if it's calling to me. In truth every inch of them calls to me.

We're kindred spirits that have met in the most unlikely of places.

Usually, when I tell someone about my gift-the gift I inherited from the women in my family-they react skeptically. I grew up talking about this kind of thing on a regular basis with my mom, which is

---

[11] Grandma; in Spanish
[12] Marigold; in Nahuatl

normal in a lot of Latine families. I never got why westernized cultures had such a hard time with it. I can't imagine growing up in a home where the other plane wasn't discussed, where you didn't believe that those who had passed could still visit and guide you. Metztli doesn't just get it, they live it. I am so thankful that I have them here. With their help I think I'll make it back home one day.

They're right, none of this is an accident. We are being watched over, and we've been brought together for a reason. *There's nothing wrong with my gift, they really are a soulmate.*

Chapter 17

The next morning my head feels heavy, and I wish I could just stay in bed. I tossed and turned all night. I kept seeing the humans being walked towards us, their unnatural smell filling my nostrils.

I move at a snail's pace as I get ready. Metzli is in the bathroom taking a shower and I reluctantly get dressed then fall back onto my bed. I'm staring at the ceiling trying to figure out how the hell I'm going to live within this cruel organization.

Before I can spiral in my horror and disgust, my mind thinks of Mya again, and the embrace she gave me right before I left our home. She held me so tight; I could feel her entire body trembling while she whispered into my ear, "Do whatever you can to get back to me, please." I know this is selfish, but I have to take part in this system, I need to make it out of here...for her. I remind myself that I am a vampire after all; anyone living like this understands that our species kills for survival and, often, enjoyment.

The next two days go by the same as the first. The only difference is, on non-feeding days, the prefects train an extra hour before we're dismissed. Once we are released for the day, we get a few hours to ourselves before curfew. Metztli and I have been having a great time getting to know each other. They remind me of two songs, "1950" by **King Princess** and "Enjoy the Silence" by **Depeche Mode**. Whenever they walk into a room, I start playing one of those songs in my head and smile, and they always wink back because they know exactly what I'm doing.

As I lay in bed and contemplate the last few days, I'm so grateful that the universe decided to send Metzli to me. I try not to tell someone everything about me the minute I meet them, but it's difficult for me. I learned the hard way that most people don't like oversharing. Not only did I lose a lot of friends by doing this in school, it also gave bullies a ton of information to berate me with. However, if I sense that I can trust someone, then I'm an open book, I tell them pretty much everything within a few days. By this time, I've told Metztli my life story—both human and vampire—and I've learned a lot about them.

I've also been observing all of the prefects and cadets very carefully. I don't connect with others easily, but I learn their traits and characteristics very quickly. The more I get to know the people here, the more I can see why The Commission watches us so closely. You can't be an arrogant jerk and work for the betterment of the group, the good of the order. Some vamps really like working for The Commission the same reason some humans choose to become cops or join the military—law and order is their thing—and they thrive in this environment. Others are serving their time out of a sincere sense of duty. I wonder how many of them are pretending, like me; I mean I get why all this is set up, but I don't like it. If I had the chance, I'd destroy The Commission in a heartbeat. Then again, I'd get rid of all vampires if I could; beings with the amount of power that we possess shouldn't exist.

On the third night I'm walking to the basement, full of self-hatred and disgust because of what I'm about to do, I wonder who I'm going to feed off of. What light we've chosen to dim so that those like us can continue to consume humanity at will. As soon as that thought pops into my head, I force it out and start playing my song. Once I'm feeding, I make sure to insert a happy event, or a pleasurable feeling. It will make no difference in the long run, and is probably really dumb of me, but I don't know what else to do; so I create beauty for them in these small moments.

Metzli and I walk to our room in silence, I feel like crap and all I want to do is crawl into bed and shut the world out. As I'm sliding into bed I think about what lies ahead. Since our three days are up I will no longer shadow Metztli. We will still room together, and they're still my go-to person when I need advice or guidance, but I will now be training with the cadets that were brought in at the same time as me. There are 20 of us, and we've been starting to introduce ourselves.

I feel nervous as I try to fall asleep. Watching the prefects was mesmerizing, their speed in combat unfathomable; knowing the accuracy needed to avoid killing each other with the slightest touch. I can't imagine ever getting to that level, especially since I think that my autistic brain has a really hard time channeling the vampire hive mind. I'm usually a second behind, or I notice everyone is doing something and I mimic, but I just don't seem to be on the same frequency as neurotypical vamps.

I've spent my whole life learning to see myself as complete and enough, but once again I'm reminded that if I'm not like everyone else-in this society-my life will be at risk here.

Chapter 18

As I'm brushing my teeth the next morning, I keep replaying my instructions in my mind. *Report to the 5th floor, room 500. Don't be late, and make sure you're prepared to train for a full day.*

I'm ready, and it's time to head out, but it's so hard to take that first step. I can tell Metztli has been watching me; as I hesitate at the door, they walk up behind me and ask, "Can I hug you?" I quickly turn around and melt into their arms. I don't like being touched unless it's on my terms, but this is exactly what I needed. I lean into them and take a deep breath; their scent is so comforting. I feel like I can reach back into their ancestry, into the Earth their family protected and tended for generations. I let go and we're both emotional; we wipe our eyes, stand up straight, and get ready for what's to come.

I walk into the training room with the false bravado I've been sporting this entire time. I don't want to come off as stuck-up or full of myself, but I do want people to know that I'm not a steppingstone. My small stature usually leads others to assume I'm not as capable. I can take advantage of this with humans, who don't expect my vamp strength and speed, but among other vampires, if I'm smaller than them, there's a good chance I'll get labeled as someone that can't hold their own.

We walk in and line up, just like we had been doing with our prefects, but now it's just us. This room looks exactly like the one the prefects train in. I like that everything here is so uniform, making it easy to adjust and focus on whatever it is I need to get done. At 2000, on the dot, our Lieutenant walks in. To my surprise, it's the man that met with me in his office the first day I checked in. I really liked his energy when I met him, so this gives me a spark of hope and confidence that I'll do okay with him in charge.

"Goodnight cadets, my name is Lieutenant Angelo, and I will be in charge of your training from now on. We will have individual trainers, who you refer to as Gunnery Sergeants, for each section. I will be overseeing the entire process. If you have any issues, go to your Gunnery Sergeant first and they will report to me. I will be watching each and every one of you, so if I have any concerns, I will meet with you to address them right away." He is standing in front of our line, right at the center as he speaks to us. "I do enjoy overseeing the training of new recruits and am looking forward to the next year with you. You may direct your eyes to the board. For this initial training, we will only have two sections open; the Virtual Reality Simulations are reserved until you have trained for a few weeks. Identify your section and report to your instructor."

I see that I'm in Section 1: Weapons. My heart skips a beat. I've really been looking forward to this. Since I first saw the training center, I've been itching to train. I may totally suck, but I'm here to learn, and I'm ready! I confidently stride over and stand in line. There are two recruits ahead of me, a young woman with long beautiful blond hair (I immediately think Rapunzel), and a short stocky guy in his late teens. We all stand at attention awaiting our orders.

A vamp who was turned at 16 steps out in front of the weapons. I still get so thrown off dealing with teenage vamps; the human side of me is like, *what's this kid doing here?!* My vamp self can sense that he's much older than me, around 100. If he wasn't a vampire, I would never suspect that he's an expert fighter; he's so lanky that, if he were human, he'd likely struggle to carry even my small frame. He's got short curly hair and piercing blue eyes that contrast with a gorgeous caramel complexion. I wonder what his life was like before he was turned. It makes me so sad to see that someone lost their humanity at such a young age, when their life had just started.

"Welcome cadets, I'm Gunnery Sergeant Michael, and I will be your weapons instructor. You will be training with me for the next two months and then you'll switch to martial arts and fighting techniques. Since vamps pick things up much faster than humans, we will spend two days learning each weapon, followed by two days of practice, and then two days of sparring. Once that six-day rotation is over, we will move onto a new weapon. We'll get through ten weapons in the course of two months." As he's talking, he's been walking up and down the line looking at each one of us before moving onto the next. When he gets to me he pauses and gets a strange look on his face, like he's made an assumption about me, and I have no idea what it is.

When I look into a human's eyes, I can see their memories, feelings, and thoughts, but not with other vampires; their energy is easy to read, but their mind is off limits. Gunny Michael's energy tells me that he is controlled and confident but fair. He's going to be a good instructor; I hope I can pick it up as quickly as they expect. He continues his explanation and lets us know that we will be learning to use Filipino fighting sticks, also referred to as escrima sticks, for our first six-day rotation. I've never heard of this weapon before, but I'm excited to try.

Gunny Michael has an assistant who starts handing out two black, wooden sticks, each about the length of my arm. Taking one in each hand, I feel an instant connection to the weapon; my instincts take over and I want to start rotating my wrists while they're in my grasp. It takes all my self-control to stand there with them at my sides, the way all of the other cadets are standing.

Gunny Michael starts showing us the foundational moves, including wrist rotations that affirm my instincts. As expected, our heightened reflexes and agility make it easy for everyone to work with the sticks. Then we start learning blocks and hits—high, mid, low. The clanking of the wood when Gunny Michael is working with someone one-on-one is so satisfying; I kind of wish I could record it and just listen to it to stim.

Even though we all learn quickly, there are still things that set us apart. Some approach this with brute force, while others are incredibly precise and stiff. I stand out because of my fluidity; I'm hitting all the spots that everyone else is but I make it look like a dance, one move flowing into the other.

As I'm training, I'm definitely playing songs in my head—I don't know if I should but I also can't help it; the movements trigger the playlist all on their own. The first song I hear is, "X.Y.U.-Take 11" by **The Smashing Pumpkins**. I spend the rest of the training session in a trance, only breaking my focus when Gunny Michael speaks to the whole group or it's my turn to train with him.

As soon as I'm left to practice the skills we just learned, I'm in the zone and the rest of the world disappears. The sticks have become a part of me, the movements come naturally, and the music flows through my limbs. At one point I notice Gunny Michael stops to watch me, I can feel him studying my every move, recognizing there's something different about me. I've never used this weapon before, but from the moment they were placed in my hands it was like they belonged there.

I act like I don't care that I'm being scrutinized and continue to practice. By the end of the day I'm still pumped, and reluctant to stop. The fact that I get to do it again tomorrow is the only thing that allows me to hand the sticks to Gunny Michael's assistant and line up with the rest of the cadets, without my brain struggling with the transition.

Throughout the whole day, Lieutenant Angelo had been stopping at each section to observe, when Gunny Michael was observing me, I could vaguely hear him and Lieutenant Angelo whispering; but I was concentrating on my movements so much that I couldn't focus on their conversation to make out what they were saying. Lieutenant Angelo now stands in front of us and says, "I'm impressed with all of you. We've got a solid group here. You are now dismissed for the day. We will see you tomorrow."

We bow and leave the room single file. As the cadets walk out, we nod to each other—the first real chance we get to acknowledge one another, since we no longer have our prefects to occupy our attention. Some cadets even pair up and start chatting. I don't really want to talk to anyone, because focusing on having a conversation would disrupt the euphoria I'm still experiencing from weapons training. I weave in and out trying to escape the group without anyone noticing. A few vamps glance my way, but no one tries to talk to me, so I'm able to slip into the elevator and head straight to my room.

When I get there I see that Metztli hasn't made it back yet; from what I've observed in the last few days, they're pretty social, so I'm sure they decided to hang out with their group for a bit. They also know that I like to be alone after a long day of interacting, and that I won't mind not having them to talk to when I finish training.

I lay down in bed and stare at the ceiling while I replay the day in my head over and over. I go over each technique I learned, what the moves looked like, the instructions Gunny Michael gave while demonstrating them, and how my body felt while I practiced. I don't know how long I lay there playing it in my mind but, before I know it, Metztli's walking into our room, "Hey, you look happy. Is it okay if I turn the light on?"

I slowly sit up, tearing myself away from my memories. "Yeah, no problem. Oh my gosh, Metztli! Today was amazing!" All of a sudden, I'm talking a mile a minute. "I got the weapons section and we learned escrima sticks, it was so cool, and I'm good at it! Gunny Michael kept giving me weird looks, and he and Lieutenant Angelo were whispering about me at some point, but that's normal right? Like they're sizing us up?"

Metztli's been undressing and getting ready for bed while I'm saying all of this. "Yeah, that's standard. They start to rank you; the rankings will then allow them to create new groupings after you've had a rotation at each section. Then they'll pair you according to your abilities. They want the strong fighters together, and they keep the weaker ones grouped so that they can focus on their gaps." Relief floods over me to have my assumptions verified by someone I admire and trust.

Now that Metzli's answer has put me at ease I stand and get ready for bed, then slide into my covers with a huge smile on my face. Eager to go to training tomorrow, I hope to fall asleep as fast as possible so that night will come sooner. I put on my headphones and enjoy "Bloody Mary" by **Lady Gaga**, which matches my mood perfectly right now.

Chapter 19

We work with the escrima sticks for the next five days, with every day just as wonderful as the first. I continue to improve my skills and realize that using the sticks gives me the same satisfaction as stimming. The movements feel so natural that it's hard to stop at the end of the day, but I'm comforted and excited by the opportunity to train the next day.

On the seventh day we are introduced to the bo staff; while I enjoy it, and show aptitude with this weapon as well, it doesn't compare to what I felt with the sticks. I'm a little bummed that I can't use them again for a long time, due to the rotation schedule. So, I go out on a limb at the end of the eighth day. As Gunny Michael finishes going over his final comments to the group, I raise my hand. "Cadet V, you may speak," he says in the formal manner which we have all become accustomed to.

The other cadets turn to stare at me. They've all started making friends within the group, but I haven't really connected with anyone. I can feel uneasy energy coming from them, judgement, even a little jealousy.

I'm so happy with Metzli's friendship that I don't feel like I need anyone else. Unfortunately, meeting people in a group setting is also hard for me. When numerous people are talking at the same time I try to listen to every conversation. As a result, I can't get a sense of an individual person's energy because I'm bombarded by too many at one time, which is both frustrating and exhausting. Nonetheless, I continue to try hanging out in groups, only to end up sitting there, mostly silent, watching everyone else interact. Most people just think I'm shy and, since there are plenty of recluse vampires, I doubt that anyone holds this against me. But because I'm so quiet, it is surprising that I am the first cadet to ever ask a question.

"Gunnery Sergeant Michael, are we able to come into the training room after we are dismissed? If I wanted to stay afterward to practice, am I able to?" I nervously wait for the response.

He stands there staring at me, giving me that same strange look he had when he examined me on day one, *I wish I knew what he was thinking!* After a minute, he finally answers.

"You are more than welcome to train as long as you want. We don't want you to burn out, but we have had incredibly dedicated cadets that enjoy putting in extra hours. As you know, this room is always monitored so you are being watched, but you are able to use any of the equipment that you have received training in."

I nod. "Thank you, Gunnery Sergeant Michael." The rest of the cadets get into their single file line and walk out, but I don't follow. A few turn back and look at me, one cadet in particular seems as if he's snarling as his dark beady eyes bore into me. *What's his problem? I didn't do anything to him.* He quickly whips his head around and I'm staring at the back of his dark brown hair, hoping I haven't already started to piss people off.

Now that I know it's an option, I decide that, each day, I'll stay at least an hour and work with the escrima sticks. All throughout training today, I kept looking at them hung up on the wall, aching to hold them and wishing I could use those instead of the bo. If I have to live in this Godforsaken place, kill innocent people, and be forced to pretend I'm something I'm not, I need to throw myself into something that will consume me. I'm hoping this weapon is what I'm looking for.

I take the fighting sticks off the wall, feeling complete as soon as they're in my hands. I automatically start to twirl them; my body reviewing every move and maneuver I've learned without any conscious effort. As my arms flow through the different techniques, the rest of my body glides across the floor, dodging and countering attacks from invisible assailants.

While I'm practicing all of this, my mind conjures the most kickass playlist, starting with "Falling" by **Opia** and **Whethan**. As I'm working with the escrima sticks, the more I practice, the more they become part of me. I even start to add my own kicks, and spins, beyond what I learned in training. Whether replicated from memory, or improvised, each motion feels so right, and I'm able to shut the rest of the world out, the way I do when I dance.

Beep...Beep! Beep...Beep! *Shit! The curfew bell. Oh shoot! I've been here for three and a half hours. Looks like I have a new special interest.*

Whenever I develop a special interest, I hyper-fixate on it—all I want to do is think about it, act on it, learn about it, talk about it. I become so engrossed that, without Mya reminding me to eat, I could go weeks without a meal, and not even notice. (Since I only ate once a week, going that long without eating wasn't as drastic as it would be for a human, but it still wasn't good for me). After a few months I'll continue to love that interest, but it no longer consumes all of my time and focus.

I put the sticks away and head towards my room. I'm smiling because it's always super fun to unlock a new special interest. Within a few weeks I may be better than the instructors. I'm not saying this because I'm conceited, when something becomes a special interest my brain doesn't rest until I've become an expert. Once I'm good at it I love teaching others about it. L.A. vamps used to get so annoyed with me because they didn't want to talk about social justice issues, the environment, or Dungeons and Dragons (just to name a few); all they wanted to do was get drunk, drink blood, have sex, and spend a ridiculous amount of money on stupid things. So, I made a lot of online friends.

Social media has a reputation for being a toxic environment, but it doesn't have to be, if you find the right crowd. I have connected with some of the most supportive, caring people online. None of them know I'm a vampire, of course, and who knows—some of them may be vamps too. All I know is that we had common goals and interests that brought us together, and for that I was always grateful. A sad smile spreads across my face as I think about how much I miss talking to them. When I told my online friends that I was going to disappear for a while due to personal issues, everyone was so caring and worried. I wish I could share all of this with them now.

As I continue to reminisce, I open the door to my bedroom. On the other side, I find Metztli standing there frozen, staring at me, they're mid step and it looks as if they've been pacing. "Where the hell have you been? I've been worried sick!" They rush up to me and grab my arms. "When you didn't show up I thought maybe you were in the library. Then an hour passed, then two, and three—and still nothing! I didn't want to ask anyone in case you were doing something you shouldn't be, and then I'd have to rat you out!" With every word they speak they shake me. "You can't scare me like that!" They're working to control their volume but the anger and frustration in their voice is obvious.

I stand there stunned; I knew we were close, but I didn't know they worried about me this much. "I...I'm so sorry, I asked Gunny Michael if I could stay behind and train some more and he gave me the okay. I was only going to stay for an hour, but I lost track of time and before I knew it the curfew bell was ringing."

They rub their temples with the tips of their fingers and let out a groan. "Are you kidding me? You were training? Here I am thinking you've decided to escape, or you're having an affair with another cadet, but my little nerd is just doing extra homework. You really keep me on my toes, V." As they say this they chuckle with exasperation. Part of them finds humor in the whole situation, and the other part is still reeling from the adrenaline my disappearance caused.

It's interactions like these that I have a hard time with. *Should I apologize? Are they mad at me? Are they making fun of me?* They can see the confusion on my face and realize I'm having a hard time processing their feelings. I'm still awkwardly standing in front of the door and don't know if it's okay to move. Metzli steadies their voice and calms their tone.

"V, I'm not upset with you. I'm sorry I came on so strong, I was just scared." They lead me to their bed, and we sit on the edge, looking at each other. "I'm sorry if I'm acting like your parent. I've just only had one other person in here that I've felt this close to, and I don't ever want anything to happen to you."

This makes more sense. They were worried about me and that led to fear, then anger. "I'm sorry I worried you, but I promise you don't have to protect me so much. I'm doing really well in my sessions, and I'll never do anything stupid." As I'm saying this irritation begins to creep into my voice. "You can stop being so controlling, I am a grown

134

woman." I'm a little hurt as I say this last line because I do feel as if they're overprotective, like they baby me. I know I'm not like everyone else, but they don't need to treat me like I can't take care of myself. I walk away from them and sit on the edge of my bed to wait for their response. I don't feel like being near them right now.

As I walk away they watch me, their instinct is to follow but they can also tell I need space. After hesitating for a moment, they walk over and sit on my bed but at the far corner to give me as much space as possible. Their voice has softened and is full of guilt as they respond, "V, that is not my intention at all. I know you think I'm treating you differently because of your disability, but I promise you that's not it. I need to tell you something." They've turned their body to face me, and their right knee is resting on the bed. They start to reach out to hold my hand, but they hesitate and decide to put their hands in their lap.

"When I'd been here for three months I became friends with another cadet in my group. She had a fire inside of her unlike anyone I'd ever met. I started to fall for her, and she felt the same about me. Our Lieutenant started to notice the glances, the playful touches." As they're recalling all of this a faint smile forms across their full lips, there's a veil over their eyes, they must be picturing her. "He pulled us aside one day and let us know that cadets dating was strictly against the rules because it made things too messy, and this place thrives on order. I don't know why they don't tell us this earlier; maybe if They let us know it's banned from the beginning, more of us would pursue secret relationships–you know how vamps love forbidden romance." At this point the intensity in their voice is growing and they stand up, they're slowly pacing in between our two beds as they look at the gray concrete floor.

"But I'm a rule follower—always have been, always will be. So, I told her we could still be friends, but I couldn't go against our Lieutenant's orders. She became so angry-not at me-but at this place, at The Commissioners. She started talking about us running away, and I kept trying to convince her that there was no way we'd make it." At this point Metzli's voice has become louder and their frustration is painful to witness. Their hands are moving at their sides as if they're still pleading with the cadet that lives within their memories.

"Even if we got out of this compound, The Commission exists all over the world, and They'd find us. I asked her to be patient, assuring her that we could be together once we were discharged from our service; after all, ten years is nothing for a vamp. She agreed, but later on I found out that it was just to appease me. In retrospect, I think something snapped when I told her we couldn't be together until we were released." Metzli's stopped moving and is just staring at the gray wall on the right side of our beds. Their long arms are hanging at their sides and the pain in their voice is palpable. *They blame themselves for all of it.* I close my eyes at this realization, I know exactly how they feel. A teardrop slowly rolls down my cheek.

After a moment's pause they continue. "One night I awoke to sirens, and we all started running out of our rooms. It was so chaotic. I tried looking for her, but she wasn't in her room and her prefect had no idea where she was." They've now turned to me and the chaos that they describe in their memory is building within them, I can see the air around them buzzing.

"The Commissioners rounded us up in one of the training rooms; They announced that a cadet had tried to escape but reassured us that the issue had been 'dealt with,' before dismissing us back to our rooms. I knew instantly that They were talking about her, and that I would never see her again. After that, I decided not to get close to anyone while I lived here. It wasn't worth it."

Their shoulders slump as they speak this last line in resignation. This event has broken them. I want to walk up to them, hold them, take all of this away but I'm stuck to my bed. I can't move and I don't know what to say.

"When you and I developed this deep connection, I instinctively became protective over you. I'm sorry, I promise I didn't mean to make you feel inferior." The haze has cleared from their eyes and they're looking right at me now. Their eyes are pleading for me to forgive them.

They look down at their hands, shame filling their voice. My brain finally releases me and I'm able to stand and walk up to them. I place my fingers under their chin and lift their face up to look at me. "You have nothing to apologize for, I would have done the same as you if I'd been through that. Thank you so much for trusting me with that story." I then gently kiss them on each cheek and finally their forehead. As I kiss their forehead they close their eyes and press into me. We embrace and I hold them until they're ready for me to let go.

There aren't any cameras in our room so as long as we're in by curfew we don't actually have to go to sleep. Although our vampire bodies do feel the pull to rest as soon as the sun comes up, we can ward it off if we want to. We stand for an hour, unmoving, holding each other tightly. I can feel Metztli's pain so deeply, it's as if my own heart has been torn apart by that event. Despite their strength and resilience, they have never gotten over this, and they likely will live with this pain for eternity. After an hour, they pull away and climb into their bed without saying a word. I go into mine, letting the white comforter envelop me as Metztli's heartbreak lingers in my mind.

When we get up the next night we don't need to say anything. After a few weeks together each of us is beginning to get a deep understanding of the other. Last night continued to solidify the bond we have been forging. Nothing like trauma to bring two people together. I've gotten a profound understanding of Metzli and they've been able to unload a huge burden they've been carrying. After we're dressed we put our foreheads together, inhale each other's scent with closed eyes, and prepare for another night.

Chapter 20

I continue in this pattern of training for the next ten sessions. I learn a variety of weapons and I'm adept at the others. I can't stand knives though, it's awkward and I feel clumsy whenever I hold one; the sticks will always be my first choice. I come up with a schedule so I don't worry Metztli. On the days that we don't feed, I stay after for two hours to work with the sticks; since I lose track of time when I practice, and I'm not allowed to bring my device to training to use as a timer, Metzli comes to meet me at the end of my allotted time.

The day before we switch to martial arts and combat training, we're working with swords. Although it's an antiquated weapon, They want us well versed in EVERYTHING. Once we're in the field there's no telling what kind of training and skills a rogue vampire will have. As I spar with one of the other cadets, I hear someone clear their throat. We both stop and I turn around to see Lieutenant Angelo a few paces away, watching me. His small stature of about 5'4" always surprises me since he has such a commanding presence. His hands are behind his back and he casually and confidently strides over.

"Cadet V, please come with me. I have already informed Gunnery Sergeant Michael, and he is well aware that I need to meet with you. You will return once we are done." I nod my head and follow him. I start thinking through every action I've taken, every word I've said in this place. *What did I do? What did I do?* When we first started he said that if there was a problem he'd be the one to deal with it. Did someone tell on me? There's nothing to tell though, I've followed every single rule while with the cadets. Shit, is it Metztli? Could they have been spying on me this whole time, have they told everything I've trusted them with to Lieutenant Angelo?

He walks me to his office without saying a word. It's the same office I came to the first day I arrived. Nothing has changed; it's as clean and empty as it was a few weeks ago. He motions to the single chair in the room, "Please sit, cadet." I sit down confidently, a calm expression on my face.

"I'm sure you're wondering why I've called you up here. We have watched you stay after your training sessions to work with the escrima. We have noticed how hard you work and your extreme dedication. You are incredibly focused and talented. It's a surprise to find this in someone who was recruited and did not volunteer, but not unheard of." His hands are folded in front of him and the intensity in his gaze makes it hard for me to fake eye contact.

"Gunnery Sergeant Michael has been keeping a close eye on you since the first day he met you. He is one of our best trainers and he can spot talent from the moment he sees a cadet." The Lieutenant's eyes glimmer and the right side of his lips turns up. "The Commission is incredibly pleased with your work. We are beyond content with your performance, and we want you to know that you are on your way to being recommended for a Spec Ops Unit." He pauses to take in my reaction, but I sit as still and confident as ever. "If you continue to show this amount of commitment and aptitude after your year of training, you will not become a prefect. Instead, you will get transferred to a special facility where you will complete your training. In your group of cadets you are the only one who is currently being recommended for this program." His hands are pressed flat against his desk and the intensity in his eyes is mesmerizing. He's pulled the golden ticket, and it's me.

I'm listening to all of this stunned; I would have never guessed he called me up here to congratulate me. I also feel a tremendous amount of guilt for suspecting Metztli. Although they've done nothing but love and support me from the moment I got here, a part of me never really let my guard down. I quickly push all of these feelings away because I have to keep up my perfect cadet ruse. "I am honored, Lieutenant Angelo. I never realized how fulfilling it would be to serve The Commission. Now that I am here, I have found a true sense of purpose, and a great desire to learn and prepare for my career within this institution."

The Lieutenant nods. "All of this is apparent in your hard work and commitment. We don't play favorites here, but we also believe in rewarding those who deserve it. If you continue to impress us, you will always have a place within The Commission."

My hands are perfectly still at my sides and my rigid composure is in line with the person I've created here. "Thank you, sir. I am grateful for yours and Gunnery Sergeant Michael's guidance. My improvement is a true testament to your program." I know I'm laying it on thick, but I can tell he's lapping it up—vamps love getting their egos stroked, and that happens to be one of my specialties. I know exactly what to say to get into anyone's good graces.

The Lieutenant stands and holds his hand out. "Know that my door is always open to you, Cadet V. I told the cadets to report to their Gunnery Sergeant with any needs, but you now have a personal invitation to come straight to me with any requests, issues, or questions."

I shake his hand firmly with so much respect. "Thank you, sir. I have nothing to report as of now, but I will come to you if the need arises." I bow and make my way out the door. Before I leave, I glance at the clock on his wall and realize that it's dismissal time. "Sir, where should I report to?"

Checking the time, he responds, "Your class is currently heading to their rooms. You are excused to prepare for feeding. I will let Gunnery Sergeant Michael know that you were with me until dismissal." I nod and continue out the door.

As I'm walking to my room I can hardly contain myself. *I'm a fuckin' badass! The Lieutenant has been watching me!* I can't wait to tell Metztli. I rush into our room and find them sitting on their bed with their back resting against the headboard, reading a book. I run over and jump onto their bed, squealing with utter delight.

They laugh and ask, "What's gotten into you?"

I'm flapping my hands, so excited that I can hardly talk. I tell them everything that happened from when the Lieutenant came into the training room until now.

The moment I start talking they sit up in their bed, leaning forward. As I talk they cover their mouth with their hands. When I'm done they drop back against their metal headboard and exclaim, "Fuckin' A, they're watching you for Spec Ops? That's MAJOR, V! Every year there are only a couple of vamps that are chosen. Shit, girl, you always told me you loved training, but I didn't know you were that good!" They sound shocked, but I can tell they're proud of me too.

"I wasn't keeping anything from you. I didn't know I was that skilled either. I just really like practicing and learning new things, and the sticks are so much fun I don't even think about it when I'm using them! I don't think it's just my skills though, you're a better fighter than me, I think it's that it seems as if I've made training my whole life."

Suddenly I remember the conversation I was not looking forward to having, I pause and think for a second. I look down and stare at my shoes, even though I don't make eye contact anyway, when I feel guilty, I'm unable to even look near a person's face. "I need to confess something to you though, when I was called to meet with the Lieutenant I was convinced I was in trouble. For a moment I wondered if you had betrayed me, if you'd told them that I sympathized with humans, how I have to stim to feed from them, and that I'm autistic. I'm sorry." I still can't look up as I say this.

"V, you don't have to apologize. Those first few weeks with you, I kept wondering if the connection I felt with you was real, or just a result of your gift... I questioned everything you said and did, because I didn't believe someone could actually be as genuine and honest as you were being." They sit up and put their right hand on my shoulder and stroke it with their thumb. "You never know who you can trust when you're around vamps, especially here, so I understand your suspicions, and I don't hold it against you at all. From now on, though, we do need to promise to never doubt one another." As they say this last sentence, they do our now-common friendship action of putting their forehead to mine.

"I promise," I say, closing my eyes and pressing my forehead into theirs in return. We sit like this for a few seconds before breaking away to report for feeding.

We make our way down to the basement, giddy with my current situation. I can feel the excited energy coming off them and I'm holding myself back from smiling. I'm not super grumpy around the other cadets but I also don't walk around smiling for no reason. I don't want to bring unnecessary attention to myself and want to blend in the way I usually do during feedings.

We walk into the room trying to act as normal as possible and take our places in line. As we're standing at attention I keep replaying my conversation with the Lieutenant over and over again in my head. Who would have known I'd be so good at all of this? This place is still complete bullshit, but it does feel good to finally feel like I can do something right.

Once everyone is lined up, the humans start to file in. It's a new batch. As usual, they're under compulsion, but this group looks healthy and scar-free, so this is the first time they've been fed on. Suddenly, my mouth starts to water, and my pupils dilate, all joy drains from my body, and I want to scream.

What the hell are you doing here, Baby Boy?

Chapter 21

I start to scan their faces, while forcing the rest of my face and body to remain still. As Madís walks through the door, it takes everything within me not to rush to him. His eyes are glazed over, he's wearing the white scrubs, and he doesn't have his glasses, but I'm certain that it's him.

My jaw tenses while I figure out what to do; he makes his way to the spot two cadets away from me. In the seconds before they're in place, I have a plan. With no time to second-guess myself, I reach into my pocket and grab one of my earbuds; it slips out of my grasp and rolls toward Madís and his assigned cadet, I raise my hand quickly and the officer on duty looks my way. "Cadet V, is everything OK?"

"Officer Jameson, I'm so sorry, but I seem to have dropped my earbud by cadet Frank's feet," I stammer, motioning to where it's laying on the ground. "Would it be alright if I retrieve it? Once I pick it up I can just file in line next to him in order to not disrupt things further." The rest of my words come out in a flustered rush. I doubt that he'll be moved by my embarrassment, so I'm really banking on the fact that news has already started to spread of me being the golden girl this year, and I start to receive special treatment.

My hunch is correct because the Officer gives me a small smile and says, "You may proceed, cadet, just be more careful next time."

I jog over, pick up my earbud, and file in next to cadet Frank. As I do this I register a silent scoff, I don't have time to figure out which cadet it came from and I keep walking as if I don't notice.

Since Frank slides to the left I'm able to take my place right next to Madís. He doesn't move or acknowledge me, locked in the mental prison They've created for him. Officer Jameson gives the commands, "Step forward, you may begin to feed."

Time is of the essence so I quickly sink my teeth into Madís. I've gotten to the point where I don't have to use my auditory stimming to control my feeding anymore. Concentrating on what I want to give to the recipient has allowed me to morph my abilities. If I'm transporting them somewhere else or allowing them a moment of peace I can keep their memories at bay and give them a respite while I drink. I enter into Madís' mind and we find ourselves on a beautiful little *rancho*. Everything is green as far as the eye can see, lush trees and vegetation surround us, and just down the little hill we're sitting on is a small house made of grey and brown rocks with a reddish roof. There's a large orange tree to its left, and a brown horse grazes off to the right.

They look around, dazed. "V, what are you doing here? Why are we at my grandparents' ranch in Michoacan?" Their brain is trying to remember what's happened, trying to process what they've been through. The pain starts coming in waves and I can't do anything to help them.

"Madís, I need you to listen to me. I know this is all confusing, you're scared, and nothing makes sense, but I don't have a lot of time. Will you be able to take in what I say?" Their hands rub their knees as they gently rock, but they nod yes, so I continue. "I don't know how, but you've been captured by a military operation run by vampires. You're being held captive in order to feed the vampires that work for this organization. You will be fed on every week and, if I don't figure something out, you will die here in a matter of months." I'm saying all of this as quickly and as clearly as I can.

They look at me, their beautiful brown eyes searching my face. "If I'm in danger, why are you here?"

My heart sinks, but I continue, "I'm currently feeding on you. I'm part of this institution. It's a long story, and I can't elaborate right now, but I made sure to be the one to feed on you so that I could talk to you inside of your mind. I transported us here so that you'd hopefully feel comfort even if just for a few minutes. Listen, I'm going to lose you any minute and I need to ask you something. If I request for you to be assigned to me would that be okay? That means that every week I would be the one to drink your blood, it would allow for me to meet and talk with you, and hopefully figure out a way out of this. I can't do it unless you give consent, I could never do that to you. I made an exception this time because I had no other choice."

I can tell there are a million things they want to say—they're terrified, angry, they want answers. But there just isn't any time, and they realize this. "I guess I'd rather have you drink from me than someone else, but V, this is really fucked up."

"I know." *Beep! Beep! Beep!* I pull away and our connection is instantly broken. I look at their rigid body, and hope that, wherever they are in their mind, they're finding comfort in the fact that I'm on their side. Then again, they've never really trusted me; for all I know, he may think I'm full of shit.

The humans are led out and our line follows once the last one exits. Metztli finds me, a big smile still on their face, but as soon as they approach they can tell something's wrong. My entire demeanor has changed, I don't want to talk, and I'm all business. We walk to our room in silence. Once the door closes behind us, I start to pace, running my hands through my hair, wishing I could pull it all out.

"What's wrong V? Is it the earbud thing? It was silly, but you're the teacher's pet now, no one will even remember it tomorrow." They're trying so hard to make me feel better but they have no idea.

"Do you remember Madís? The human I met in the club and then rescued from the rooftop?" I ask while still pacing.

"Yeah, yummy little baby boy. What about him?"

"He's here." I stop and look right at them.

"Shut the fuck up V, what are the chances?" They look just as stunned as I feel.

"I don't know, I don't freaking know, but I pulled that stupid earbud stunt so that I could move in line and feed on him. I was able to talk to him while I fed. I told him I'd get him out of here. I don't know what to do Metztli! What the hell am I going to do?" I crumble to the floor; tears are running down my face.

I don't know why Madís affects me so much but, from the moment I danced with him in that club it's like my heart's been tied to his. I kept telling myself it was a feeding thing; I was craving human blood and since he smelled so good I must have just kept the fantasy of feeding on him in my mind. But this is deeper than that. The moment I smelled him I had a visceral reaction; deep down inside me, my soul called to his and his soul responded.

"Metztli I'll never recover if he dies because of us. He doesn't deserve to be here—none of them do." I rest my head on my knees as I sob and start pulling at my hair. They kneel down next to me and rub my back, letting me cry. They don't say anything for a long time, simply letting me process and feel.

Once I stop making noise, they say, "We're going to figure this out, V. I don't know how right now but we've got at least three months.

This was a brand new batch and they look healthy and strong. I promise you, we're going to figure this out." They pick me up off the floor and walk me to my bed. They tuck me in and kiss me on the forehead. I've cried so much that my eyes are tired and can barely stay open. "Mmmmmmm...mmmmmmmm...mmmmmmmmmm," my humming helps to calm me. Even though my heart is shattered, and I can't think straight, my exhaustion pulls me into a deep sleep.

Chapter 22

The next night I wake up groggy, but I jolt up when I remember everything that happened the day before. I run to the bathroom and start dry heaving into the toilet; usually when this happens, nothing comes out, but this time I do throw up a good amount of blood–his blood. I walked away from him so he wouldn't be in any danger. I left him behind so he'd be safe. It wasn't supposed to be like this. Suddenly I hear the Lieutenant's voice in my head, *"Know that my door is always open to you cadet V, I told the cadets to report to their Gunnery Sergeant with any needs, but you now have a personal invitation to come straight to me with any requests, issues, or questions."* I know how to make sure that I'm the only one who feeds on Madís. Today after practice, instead of training, I'll go talk to Lieutenant Angelo.

I can hear Metzli getting dressed in our room. I stagger to the doorway with my hands on my stomach, praying that another wave of nausea doesn't hit. "Hey, I have something I need to run by you."

They bite their cheek, concern painted across their face. They easily heard me throwing up. They look up at the clock that's above their bed and answer with a furrowed brow. "We have time, shoot."

My hands are in my pockets, and I timidly explain my plan because for all I know it may be stupid. "I'm going to tell Lieutenant Angelo that feeding from Madís gave me an energy boost. Since The Commission wants me in tip top shape I'm going to ask if it's possible for me to be the only one that feeds from him whenever his unit is brought out."

They sit on the edge of their bed and contemplate what I've just said. "Hmmm, not bad. There are theories that certain humans' anatomies fit perfectly with specific vamps' biology. I've read vamp scientific journals about it, it's pretty cool. Hopefully the Lieutenant is aware of that and buys your story." They rub their eyes with their right hand, I'm stressing them out so much. "I'm here to support you in whatever you decide. *Dime lo que necesitas y siempre te ayudare,[13]*" they start to put their boots on as time is ticking and they would never be late to training.

"*Gracias hermane, no sé qué haría sin ti.[14]*" I walk over and shyly kick their boot with the tip of my toe. It isn't easy for me to let others help me, and Meztli's unwavering support makes me feel awkward every time. They look up at me and pucker their lips to send me an air kiss. *Damn, I love them.*

I head to training, but it's the worst night to have to start in a new section. It's hard to concentrate, yet I know I'm being watched closely by my new Trainer, Gunny Sophia. She's French and has a very thick accent.

I'm practicing Long One, an especially challenging form, when someone grips my wrist from behind. "I know you've gotten used to special treatment because of your exemplary dedication, but don't get sloppy, cadet."

I stop what I'm doing and turn to look at Gunny Sophia. She places a flat hand against my back. "Improve your posture, strengthen your stance. You seem distracted. When you are here I need you in complete control."

---

[13] Tell me what you need and I will always help you; said in Spanish.
[14] Thank you sibling (hermane is the gender neutral use of hermano/a), I don't know what I'd do without you; said in Spanish.

"Yes ma'am." I quickly tighten up and do exactly as she has instructed. She nods her head, pleased with my ability to take criticism, and moves on.

As I improve my stance the hairs on the back of my neck stand up, I turn and a few cadets are glancing my way, they're smirking and I can tell they enjoy that Gunny Sophia called me out. *It's okay, jealousy is normal, I didn't do anything wrong.*

Even though I dreaded working today, it actually helps distract me so that I can get through the night. The fighting style we begin with is karate; we learn the basics, commencing the same six-day training routine that we were on with weapons. I put my entire self into the session so that I can escape for at least a little bit. As soon as the day ends, I head straight for Lieutenant Angelo's office. I knock on his door and hear a buzz. I push the door open and am greeted by his warm eyes; he has a fatherly presence to him, but I simultaneously sense something dark behind that calm demeanor. He is part of The Commission, and I know I must tread lightly.

"Cadet V, it's nice to see you. I heard your first day of martial arts went well." My surprised look gives me away, "I know you just left the building, but when someone is on our radar, we make sure to keep track of their training closely," he explains calmly.

That makes sense, I guess, but it's creepy as hell too. Maybe being the rising star isn't as cool as I initially thought. I was supposed to come here, keep my head down, and get out. Now I'm being watched and scrutinized more carefully than I would have ever imagined.

Oh shoot, my mind's wandering. I need to get to business. I sit down and start to speak, masking any quiver in my voice. I run through my request to feed off of Madís and why, I don't mention their name, of course, but they keep such impeccable records I know he'll know which human I fed off of yesterday.

He puts his index finger to his nose and his thumb under his chin, considering my request carefully. "I commend you for being so proactive—most young vampires do not recognize such things. A request such as this has not been brought up before." He leans over his desk and squints as he looks deep into my eyes, "There's something different about you, but I can't quite put my finger on it." He inhales deeply and closes his eyes, he's taking my scent in. *SHIT, did I just fuck up?*

"I'm going to have you stand outside for a bit," he says, his voice cold, all warmth has drained from the room as he continues to examine me with his eyes. "I need to make a call. I will have you come back in when I'm done."

I nod and obediently rise, exit his office, and stand in the hall, my back leaning against the wall that's connected to his door. *I can't act nervous, I can't show any fear, I'm being watched as I stand here, eyes forward, back straight.* I don't know how much time passes as I stand there but it's unbearable. His office must be soundproof because I hear absolutely nothing.

The door finally opens, "You may join me once again cadet." I walk in and sit.

I sit in the chair and when I look at him, he's completely calm and collected, I can't get a reading off of him at all, it's like he's put a wall around himself. *What the hell? Is he blocking me?*

He stands behind his desk with one hand behind his back and paces back and forth. "After speaking with my superiors, I have some questions I'd like to ask before giving your request a final answer."

I'm sitting rigidly and looking straight at him. "Yes, Lieutenant."

153

"What is your vampire gift?"

He's caught me off guard. I hope my face doesn't show how scared I am right now. I don't know how much info is in my file, I don't want to say too much or too little. "It's a form of telepathy sir. My compulsion abilities are much stronger than the average vampire's. I do not have powers over other vampires, though. I am able to gauge anyone's essence and intention through my gift as well."

As I'm speaking he continues to pace and looks up at the ceiling as if he's trying to make up his mind about something. He walks around his desk and rests his body at the front of it, facing me. He leans back against his hands and smiles. The look on his face makes me uneasy. "You are well aware that I have all of that information, but I wanted to hear it from you. You've been granted a very rare opportunity, cadet, and The Commission knows more about you than you could ever imagine." His eyes widen and as he smiles I see that his fangs have descended. *What the hell is going on?*

He suddenly grabs my wrist and bites into it. I gasp but stay perfectly still, this vamp holds my life in his hands right now, I can't do anything to make things worse than I already have. He sucks three times then releases my arm and wipes a trickle of blood from the edge of his lips.

He closes his eyes and sits perfectly still for a few seconds then slowly opens them and begins to speak. "Your request, although plausible, is odd, cadet. The Commission cannot take any chances and must make sure that every cadet is fully and completely dedicated to Our cause." He slowly stands and with his index fingers at his lips goes and sits behind his desk. "My gift allows me to examine someone's blood composition, as you know, through your gift, I can't always control exactly what I receive but I am able to learn much more than just having the pleasure of tasting you." A chill runs down my spine, *creep.*

"Do you want to know what I have discovered?" His head tilts downward and his eyes narrow as he stares at me.

I breathe deeply and stay as composed as ever, "Only if you'd like to share, Sir."

"You are so well behaved; I enjoy that about you. Well, I am pleased to report that you were telling the truth. Your blood is indeed enhanced. That human's blood has bonded with yours and will indeed be an asset to your training. My superiors have given me the directive to allow your request if my test proved you were being honest with me. Congratulations, when that unit is fed from, that human will indeed be assigned to you." As he's saying all of this he looks at me with the hunger of a predator who's about to pounce. It takes everything within me to hold my composure as my stomach turns sour, and I feel like I want to throw up.

"I completely understand Lieutenant, everything we do is for the good of The Commission. Thank you for taking the time to review my request thoroughly and for allowing my appeal." I stand and face him but make no other movements.

"It pleases me that you understand our expectations so well, is there anything else I can do for you cadet?" A satisfied smile spreads across his face and for the first time I notice that the tooth behind his canine is metal.

"No sir, thank you for your continued support. I will not disappoint you." I bow and start to walk out the door.

"Cadet V?" I turn to face the Lieutenant. "We know you won't let us down because if you do it will cost you your life, and none of us wants that." I focus on the way the ground feels beneath my feet, I listen to the slightest sounds in the room, and I let my mind wander to stop myself from gagging or stimming. I walk out as calmly as I walked in, but it takes all of my willpower. I walk down the hall and into the elevator, I can't let my guard down until I'm in my room because I know that They're sure to be watching my every move and reaction.

My breathing is shaky as I step off the elevator and walk down the hall. I'm going to have to come up with a way to trick the most powerful organization in the world, and I have no idea what I'm doing. With my head down, lost in my thoughts, I walk into my room and make a beeline to my nightstand. Needing to plug in for a little bit, I pull out my device. It takes a few moments to realize that Metztli's there and they've been talking to me. I look up, pulled out of my daze. "I'm sorry, I was in my own world. I didn't even realize you were in here; what did you say?"

They look at me lovingly, with so much tenderness and worry in their eyes. "I was just checking to see if you're okay."

"No, I'm not." I then describe mine and the Lieutenant's interaction, making sure to describe every detail. My eyes are glued to the floor the entire time I speak, while I simultaneously go over possible solutions in my head. When I'm deep in thought I tend to look at the ground and pace, it's a stim that helps me process a lot of information at once.

"What a fuckin' pervert!" I look up at them and their hands are shaking at their sides, "If kicking his ass wasn't a sure-fire way to get me killed I'd be ripping his jaw out right now!"

"Metzli, it's not worth it to get all worked up, did you really think that the people in this place care about consent? This whole system is built off of forced labor." I've sat next to them in bed and I'm slowly rubbing their back trying to get them to calm down. "You know what's really wild?" I ask.

"Even wilder than your superior having feasted on your life force?"

"I guess it's all relative, but did you catch the fact that the BS story I made up about Madís making me stronger is true? Lieutenant Angelo said my blood was enhanced..." As I say this I can feel my hands begin to shake because I'm really freaked out right now, and my anxiety is mounting.

"Shit, I was so pissed about you getting assaulted that I didn't even think about that. What the hell?" Metzli's biting their bottom lip, and I can see the wheels turning in their head. "Do you feel any different after drinking his blood?"

"At this point I have no idea; my head is spinning. I was so freaked out from seeing them, and trying to figure out how to save them, that I haven't been paying attention to how I feel. I've always felt different around them, but I thought that was a lust thing. Maybe I came up with this because subconsciously we are biologically made for each other, I don't know." Huge tears are running down my face, I'm crying more out of frustration than sadness, but either way I wish I could scream right now.

Metzli wraps their arms around me and holds me, I put my head on their shoulder and close my eyes. I'm so tired; tired of always being different, tired of having to work so hard at everything. Most vampires don't give a shit about anyone but themselves, would my life have been easier if I could have been like that?

No. As hard as things have always been I don't want to lose my love for others, I don't ever want to be like Them.

Metzli interrupts my thoughts as they speak slowly, resignation in their voice, "I know the system's shit, but I'm good at fighting and I finally felt like I fit somewhere. Ignoring all the other crap was a price I was willing to pay to not feel so alone." I pull my head away from their shoulder and take their hand in mine.

I gently kiss the back of their hand and close my eyes as I inhale their scent, "Sorry I came in and blew everything up."

They put their forehead up against mine and close their eyes, "You have nothing to apologize for. I was living in a dream world, and it was about time someone woke me up."

"So, I get to be the prince in our version of Consensual Sleeping Beauty?" I ask as I try to lighten the mood.

They playfully push my shoulder and say, "You're such a smart ass."

I sadly answer, "And you love me for it. Hey, I need to plug in for a while, I'm going to zone out and then go to bed. After all of this I can barely keep my eyes open, my brain's trying to shut down." I give their thigh a squeeze and sluggishly walk over to my bed. I feel numb at this point, my brain has stopped processing and I just need to turn it all off.

"No problem, Prince Charming. If you need me let me know." They walk into the bathroom, and I hear the shower turn on. I go underneath the covers, put my headphones on, and get lost in my music. The first song that comes on is, "I Want You Around" by **Snoh**

Aalegra. I let the beat permeate deep into my mind and I get lost in her voice as I drift off to sleep.

Chapter 23

The rest of the week proceeds as usual. I find comfort and distraction in my training sessions. Even on feeding days, I head to the training center afterward. I need to stay busy in order to keep my mind occupied. Luckily, the Instructors and Lieutenant just think that my status as an exemplary cadet is what's fueling my extreme dedication. They're pleased, and I'm glad that my coping mechanisms also work in my favor. Being autistic, and my ability to mask well, has helped me out in this space.

The humans we feed from are rotated weekly, so it will be a while until I see Madís again. My heart yearns to see him and talk to him, but I have to be patient. In the meantime, I've been practicing what I'll say. I also keep wondering why he keeps being brought into all of these situations, and why it always involves me. Thinking back to Metzli's Abuela, I conclude that this can't just be bad luck. I also realize that some things are not meant to be understood until the time is right, and I know that when I am meant to comprehend all of this, I will.

It's finally the day that I get to feed from Madís. As always, I arrive to training early, continuing the role of the slightly obsessive, antisocial V that everyone has come to know. By this point, we've moved on to Jiu Jitsu. Luckily, once I'm training, I am able to immerse myself in whatever I'm learning. I replay the Gunny's instructions in my head as I practice each move, working to make them as precise and deadly as possible.

Today I'm practicing with a cadet named Samson who was turned at 17.

He walks up to me in his fighting stance with a big smile on his face. His long curly hair is tied back in a low pony. "Don't worry, I'll go easy on you chica."

I giggle, "As easy as you went on me the last time I pinned you?"

"Oh yea, I didn't use my full strength that day, I could tell you could use the win." He winks and slowly starts to circle the perimeter of the mat, his blue eyes full of mischief.

"Ha, I guess now you know I don't need special treatment, bring it on pretty boy."

We slowly approach one another and begin to weave in and out of an oh so familiar dance. Some cadets treat me with contempt and others don't mind my growing status, I'm glad Samson's of the latter.

Even though I don't hang-out with any of the cadets, I am friendly during training. I don't have time to make friends but I don't want to be a jerk either. I'm an expert people watcher, it's how I learned to mask so well. I'm able to learn about others through the simplest of observations, and being capable of reading their energy gives me a huge advantage also. It makes it so that although I'm not overtly friendly I can act cordial with all of the cadets in my unit.

While we're sparring, I notice that Gunny Sophia is watching me, a slight smile on her face. I'm impressing her and living up to their expectations...*perfect.*

An hour away from dismissal, I feel like I want to crawl out of my skin. I'm weighed down by the anticipation of seeing Madís and the worry of not knowing what to say to him. The hour drags on, feeling more like three by the time we're lining up. I head to my room and find that Metztli is already there, since they always like to shower before feeding. Instead of speaking to them, I just sit on my bed and close my eyes, remembering the Madís I met at the club. Their young, confident, angelic face was so full of life. "I promise I'll get you out of here..." I whisper, as I breathe deeply and try to clear the lump that has formed in my throat.

I sit there meditating and preparing for one of the toughest things I've ever had to do. When I fed from him last time I had to completely ignore his scent, his taste, and the feel of his blood in my system. Every part of him calls to me, and when I'm with him, I'm able to fill a gap that nothing—not the escrima sticks, not Mya, nor Metzli— has ever been able to satisfy.

I've decided to try something new tonight, and all I can do is hope that it works. My thoughts are interrupted as Metzli walks out of the bathroom, "You ready?" they ask.

"No, but I don't have a choice." I walk up to them and rest my head against their chest, they rub my back with both hands and kiss the back of my head.

"I got you girl, you can do this." I nod, take a deep breath, and walk to the door.

We head down and line up in the basement as usual. This time, however, there is already an officer waiting when I walk in. He locks eyes with me as soon as I enter before walking over. "Cadet V, Lieutenant Angelo has informed me that, once a week, you will stand at the front of the line. Follow me." I walk to my spot and eagerly await Madís' entrance, but I make sure to exude none of that excitement.

As I'm walking to my spot the stares are apparent. As I walk by cadet Erik I notice his eyes narrow and the hateful energy radiating from him tries to suck me in. He's despised me from the moment I started standing out. *Fuck you Erik.*

Once we're all in place, the door opens to Madís at the head of the line. In one week, they've transformed, nobody else would believe they are the same person. They've lost all their spark, their gaunt, pale frame and sluggish persona, just a foggy memory of what they used to be. I'm saddened, but not surprised; humans aren't meant to be under compulsion for this long. A vamp's control doesn't just drain a person of their blood—it kills their spirit and depletes their essence.

As soon as they stop in front of me, I step forward. When I'm given the okay, I sink my teeth into their shoulder, avoiding the wound from last week, and instantly work at controlling their mind. This time I take them to the outside of the club where we met. There's nothing else like L.A. at night, and it's just the two of us. When we first arrive, I can tell that they're in pain, feeling what their body is going through in real time.

"Let go of the pain, listen to my voice..." I lift their face to mine and look deeply into those precious angelic eyes. As they're looking at me their pupils start to focus, and the tension in their body is slowly released. I play "Halo" by **Beyonce** in the background to calm them, which seems to work. They reach out and grab my hands, lowering our intertwined fingers to our chests. Madís stares at me, and I smile. In this space they look the way I remember them, short brown silky soft hair, their creamy complexion that reminds me of *cafe con leche*[15] looks good enough to eat.

Then, out of nowhere, they push me with all their might. I stumble backwards, caught off guard. I stop the music and look up at

---

[15] Coffee with milk; in Spanish.

them, only to be met with so much rage and hatred. Too disgusted to look at me, they turn around before shouting, "You're a monster! How the hell can you do this to people? I get that vampires need to feed, but you have no idea what it's like to live like this!"

I stay where I am because they have every right to detest me. "Madís, turn around and look at me." Surprisingly, they do, but the scorn on their face cuts me deeper than I thought it would.

"I know we're monsters. That's why I kept pushing you away. I knew that if I got close to you, your life would be full of pain and death. I was turned against my will; I didn't choose to be what I am! I was also forced to come here. I guess I could have taken my life in order to refuse to partake in this system, but I admit that I wasn't willing to go that far." My right hand is pulling my hair back while my left is squeezing my shoulder. How am I going to help him if he hates me?

"I'm doing everything I can to figure out how to get you out of here. I'm starting to make a name for myself here, and I think I'll be able to use that to my advantage in order to save you." He's turned away from me at this point so I'm talking to his back. "You can hate me for the rest of your life, but I'll die making sure yours doesn't end here. I know that there's nothing I can say to make any of this okay. I just need for you to trust me because, when it's time for me to help you escape, you need to do exactly as I say."

They sit on the edge of the sidewalk and look out into the distance. I take a tentative step toward their turned back. "Can I sit down without you punching me? It won't hurt me, but I want to respect your space if you don't want me near you."

Looking at the stained concrete next to him, he replies flatly, "Go for it."

164

I realize that the plan I've formed in my room is working. I've been manipulating time the way our mind is able to in dreams. In the real world ten minutes may pass but in your subconscious, it can feel as if hours have gone by. We've been talking for longer than five minutes and I haven't heard the monitor ring yet. *Sometimes it's the small victories,* I think to myself, grateful that at least one thing went in my favor.

We sit there in silence; I don't try to talk and I don't expect him to, either. After what feels like an eternity, he finally speaks. "When I first met you, you were all I could think about. I saw you in my dreams. When I closed my eyes not only could I see you, but I could smell you. I thought I'd found my soulmate, I started looking for you online, desperate to find out who you were." He rubs his forehead and shakes his head in a way that screams, *I'm such an idiot.*

"Then when you walked into that party, I thought my prayers had been answered—I couldn't believe my luck. But after all that vampire shit went down, I swore I'd stay as far away from you as possible." They start to tap their fingers against their thigh but still refuse to look at me, "Growing up, I heard stories of the humans who'd sold their souls to the devil for eternal life. Their need to feed on human blood was a curse for immortality."

My head is turned and I'm watching their every move as they continue to speak. "Saying it out loud, it still sounds so stupid. I keep waiting to wake up from this nightmare, to realize that you aren't real, and that I dreamed the whole thing up. Instead, the terror of it all just seems to get worse."

He finally looks at me and says, in a small voice, "I'm scared V, I'm really, really scared." They start to cry, and I reach out and cradle their head to my chest. I let them sob as long as they need to, running my fingers through their hair and softly singing, "La Sandunga", a song my mom used to sing to me when I was a child and didn't feel well. I want to tell them that I think we are soulmates but it's all too much for them right now.

He starts to become one with me, and I rock him back and forth to the melody. As I'm doing this, I start to get tired; I've used a lot of energy doing all of this, and I don't want to just leave him. I let go and he slowly sits up.

"Madís, I've been using my vampire gift to control your mind when I feed. I don't know how much longer I can hang on, though. Pretty soon we're going to hear a beep. When that happens, all of this will disappear, I will disappear, and you'll go back to the physical and mental prison that you're in. I'll see you again next week, and I just need you to fight like hell, and hold on. Can you do that for me, Baby Boy?"

The fear in their eyes is too much to bear. I want to look away, but I won't do that to them, I won't ever turn away from them. "Yeah, I can do that." As they answer their voice is low and I can tell they're holding back more tears.

"Good." I give them a melancholy smile.

"V, I'm sorry I got so angry at you. You keep saving me and instead of thanking you, I keep insulting you." They're looking at their feet; I can tell apologizing isn't their strong suit.

"I'm not offended. Trust me, I know vampires are a bunch of asshats. Just promise me that, once I get you out of here, you learn to stay out of trouble." I say this with a playful smile on my face and, right before the timer goes off, I hear them giggle softly.

Chapter 24

After feeding, I head straight to my room, crawl into bed, put my headphones on, and get ready to fall asleep. I'm completely drained after all the effort it took to do that, and I can barely keep my eyes open. The last thing I remember is listening to "I Would Hurt a Fly" by **Built to Spill**, and then darkness.

The next night, I wake up feeling like I have the worst hangover in the history of drinking. My head is pounding, it's hard to see clearly, and every little sound bombards my system. Vampires don't get sick so I can't even fake an illness to skip training. The best I can do is take a cold shower; although it does clear my mind a little, I am still in bad shape. I look in the mirror and I even look hungover; my eyes are bloodshot, and the vein at my temple is visible and pulsing. I walk out of the bathroom and Metztli exclaims, "Whoa, you look horrible!"

"Thanks, I love you too," I shoot back sarcastically, as I fall back onto my bed.

"No seriously, you look really bad. You can't go to practice like this, they'll know something's up. You really messed yourself up going into that kid's head yesterday." They start to pace.

"I know, but it was worth it, and I'm going to do it again." As I say this, I close my eyes and picture Madís. I know their life is in danger and I'm trying to figure out how to outsmart a million-dollar worldwide corporation—*but damn, he's fine*. I smile as I remember their olive skin, and perfect pink lips.

"You're not risking your life just to get into that human's pants, are you? Cause you look horny as hell right now, and I can only imagine what's going through your mind." Metztli smirks, only half-joking.

"I'm not that stupid, but I also can't help that I want to do some really naughty things with them, they're so fucking adorable!" We chuckle a little, before I sit up and look at Metzli earnestly. "Silliness aside, we need to get today figured out."

They continue to pace as they think, before turning abruptly to look at me. "Listen, some vamps just have a hard time living in captivity. We are made to be hunters, after all. I've seen vamps get super messed up from being trapped here, it's almost like they go into a depression." They've sat down at their desk and are holding their chin in their hands as they continue thinking out loud.

"Luckily, They have protocols in place to keep us from losing ourselves. As your prefect, it's my job to report if I suspect that the environment is messing with you." They quickly glance up at the clock. "I have just enough time to go talk to my Lieutenant about it. If I don't come back in twenty minutes it means they bought it and you can stay here and rest." They start walking to the door and pause with their hand on the doorknob. "You need to go back to sleep because it should only take your body one day to recover, and then you need to return to your usual activities tomorrow, I'll wake you if I need to. Sound good?" They ask, obviously proud of their plan.

"You're a genius! I guess your good looks aren't the only reason I keep you around." I tease, standing up to give them a quick hug before crawling back into bed. They walk over and pull the covers over me before walking out the door. I sleep all night and don't wake until I hear them return. I sit up, still drowsy, but eyes halfway open and directed at Metzli. "Fill me in, what did they say?"

They excitedly summarize, "It was so easy. I shared that I noticed signs of confinement sickness—that's what I've heard it called—

168

and that I thought you needed a day to rest. The Lieutenant was extra concerned since you are their shining star this year. She did say that tomorrow you need to report to the Vamp Doc, so start building your story."

They head into the bathroom and continue talking while they're washing up. "Is it cool if I go hang out with my group? If you want me here, I'll totally stay, but I thought you'd just want to sleep."

"Yeah, of course. I wanted to hear what you had to say but I'm going to continue to rest. Thanks for being so amazing, I'll see you tomorrow night." I close my eyes, and hear the water turn off, then feel Metztli kiss me on the forehead before they head out the door.

The next night I wake up and I feel like myself again. My energy is normal, I look rested, and I'm ready to train. I do have to check in with the Vamp Doc, but I'm not worried about that at all. I've dealt with depression my entire life, and I've seen a ton of psychiatrists, psychologists, and therapists. It won't be hard to convince the doctor that my mental health has been suffering from the confinement. Before Metztli opens the door we put our foreheads together, I take a deep breath, and I whisper, "I could never get through this without you." I feel them smile and before we head out the door they give my hand a little squeeze.

I report to training and am told that the doctor will send for me when he's ready. About ten minutes into our lesson, a Commissioner walks in, speaks with Gunny Sophia, then walks over, "Follow me Cadet V." I obediently follow but the heat from my fellow cadets' stares bore into me. *Keep your head up, stay calm, exude strength.*

He takes me to the tenth floor where we walk through an unmarked door at the end of the hall. I don't know what I expected, but it's an entire science facility, like the kind I've only seen in sci-fi movies. There are monitors everywhere, tables filled with test tubes and microscopes, and a ton of medical equipment. I failed all of my college labs, so all of this is another world to me. My escort walks me to a metal gurney and tells me to sit, then waits at the end of the bed, silent, hands behind his back, eyes facing forward.

A few minutes later, the Vamp Doc walks in, wearing a white lab coat. I'd guess that he was turned at around eighty years old, making him one of the oldest looking vamps I've ever seen. He has a white beard that's closely cut to his face, and from the moment I look at him I'm filled with a strange, uneasy feeling.

"Hello, Cadet V. Your prefect reported that you may be experiencing confinement sickness. I'm going to take your vitals and then I'll ask you a few questions." He does all the normal doctor stuff, like listening to my heartbeat, checking my pupils, and drawing some blood.

He walks to the corner of the lab where a large metal machine sits on the counter. He inserts five vials of my blood into a round hole just big enough for them to fit into. A screen on the front of the apparatus turns on and he quickly pushes a button to make it go black. I can hear the machine still humming so I know he didn't turn it off, but he didn't want me to be able to see what the tests were going to disclose.

He then walks over and sits on a stool across from me. He pulls the laptop, sitting on a small metal desk with wheels, towards him. His eyes scan the screen as he talks, "So far everything looks normal, nothing to worry about physically." He pushes the computer to the side and a quizzical look crosses his face as he examines my features. "Tell me what's been going on."

"For the past week I've been feeling wrong, but I don't know what the problem is. I get these urges to scream, to rip my skin off, but I don't know why. I'm happy here. My Gunnery Sergeants are fantastic, I love to train, I'm excited about getting chosen for the special unit. I just can't seem to control this feeling." I start to rub my pants with the palms of my hands. I'm allowing myself to stim openly as I describe how anxious I feel. "Some days I'll be walking around, and I feel like I can't breathe, which is weird because vampires don't even need to breathe. Yesterday morning my prefect noticed that I hadn't gotten out of bed yet, and when they tried to wake me I could barely open my eyes. It's like all the life had been sucked out of me, I just wanted to sleep," as I've been saying this the doctor has gone back to his laptop and has been typing and nodding.

"No need to worry, Cadet V, this is a straightforward case of confinement sickness, and nothing to be ashamed of. Vampires are not supposed to be kept in concrete communes, and your body is just craving its natural environment." As he's speaking he walks over to a small refrigerator that's on the counter behind his computer then turns to look at me. "I've heard a lot about your special talents, and it actually makes sense that you would succumb to this. Someone as skilled as yourself must be an excellent killer in the wild, so your instincts are craving that, and your mind wants to shut down without it." He opens the refrigerator and pulls out a glass vial with a metal lid, which he places next to his computer and then sits on his stool once again.

171

"I am going to prescribe an enhancement medication. Since you're a vampire, it won't harm you, and there is no fear of addiction. Our bodies do not respond to drugs the way a human body would. We heal too fast to succumb to those physical ailments. Whenever you feel yourself getting anxious, just drink 10mg from this vial." He picks the small, unmarked, amber colored bottle up and hands it to me. He then walks to a cabinet that is across the room from us and pulls out a plastic oral syringe. "If you run out, let your Lieutenant know and I will give you more. Don't worry about how often you take it, as I said before it will not harm you." While he's explaining all of this he hands me the plastic syringe. I listen carefully to his every word, and nod along like I understand the severity of all of this.

"Thank you very much, Doctor. I'm glad to hear that there is a solution." I stand and am escorted out by the Commissioner, who's been standing by the gurney the entire time. The doctor continues typing on his laptop, engrossed in whatever information he's entering. As the door is closing I think I hear him say, "Wonderful, just as We hoped." I quickly turn to look at him but the door slams in my face. Was that about me? I fucking hate this place.

I go to my room and put the vial in my dresser then head back to the training center. I continue with a full day of fighting and notice the sideways glances and whispers. It doesn't last long because they know the repercussions for envious behavior, but I can still feel it, even after they pretend that they don't care about me. I'm sure they've all been given the same lecture by their prefects that Metzli gave me. Nobody would dare say or do anything to incur The Commission's wrath. We all just want to blend in and do as we're told, *what a screwed up system.*

I head to my room to prepare for tonight's feeding but it's nothing special. I won't feed from Madís again until next week, so today will just be a random human.

After feeding, Metztli and I return to our room right away. I can tell they're eager to know what happened with the Vamp Doc; I explain everything and show them the vial. They turn it in their fingers and inspect the liquid that's inside, but they have no idea what it is either.

"The doctor said it's for enhancement, so I'm thinking it's like steroids for vampires." I shrug as I sit on my bed next to my nightstand.

Metztli turns it one last time then walks over and drops the vial in my hand while giving my palm a small squeeze. They look at me for a second longer than usual but decide to say nothing. They move to their desk, sit, and bring out the book that they're currently reading.

All of a sudden they slam the book shut excitedly and look up at me. "Hey! If that shit they gave you is like steroids for vamps, what if you take it after you mind control Madís so you can keep your energy up? Now that you have the meds you won't be able to fake confinement sickness if feeding from Madís messes you up again." Their eyes are quickly scanning the floor, I can tell they're putting all of the pieces together as the wheels turn in their mind. "Even if it doesn't work, what do you have to lose?"

"Ugh, I don't know about this Metzli, I know you're trying to help, but I got a really bad reading off of the Vamp Doc"

"I don't like this anymore than you, but it's the only thing I can think of to get you one step closer to executing your plan. I would never want to do anything to put you in danger. Do you have a better idea?"

I try to run through alternative options but they're right, I don't know what else to do. "Fuck… I can't pull this off any other way." My voice is shaky, and my lip start to quiver as I continue to speak, "If it doesn't work I won't be any worse off than if I don't take it." Now I'm closely examining the liquid, squinting, as if that will help me see something that wasn't there before. "I'll make my final decision once I feed from Madís again. Things are a little too raw for me to decide right now."

I open the drawer in my nightstand, and put the vial and syringe away, lay on my bed, and put my headphones on. I need to stim before going to sleep, this week's been so intense I'm barely keeping my anxiety in check. I start out by listening to "On & On" by **Erykah Badu**. As I lay there I can feel Metzli pausing to look up at me every few minutes. They're biting their bottom lip with their eyebrows scrunched. I wish I could tell them that everything's going to be okay, but I don't really know that.

Chapter 25

We're resting on a grassy hill full of dandelions, the sun is shining on our faces. We lay on our backs and I'm smiling as I feel the warm rays and enjoy the sunshine. *Damn, I miss doing this in real life.*

As they're relaxing I turn on my right side to face them and start to explain, "Sorry to ruin the mood, but I still have no idea how to help you escape. I'm a skilled fighter but planning for this kind of thing is not my strong suit."

Their eyes are closed as they take in the sunshine, but I can tell that they're thinking. "Lucky for you, I'm good at strategizing. I used to think I'd join the military, but when I decided I wanted to transition, I chose myself over that career. I ended up just bouncing around doing odd jobs-since I never really found something that I was passionate about. Anyway, I'm going off topic..." They roll onto their left side so that we're face-to-face. "The first thing you need to do is get the plans to this place. When they take us out of here, I'm not lucid enough to give you any info." As they say this, I'm making mental notes of how I can accomplish this, and come up with a few ideas.

"Tomorrow, after my extra training, I'll start working on this. It's funny because what you've said is so simple, but I had such a mental block I couldn't even come up with that on my own." I pause and give him a thoughtful look. "Hey, how are you doing? I'm sorry I came in here just talking strategy when you're in hell twenty-four hours a day."

He shrugs. "I've found that accepting my current state is the best way to get through it. When I'm not with you it's like I'm sitting in this white room, I'm not physically in a white room though, it's like it's been created in my mind." They sit up and while they recall all of this their face contorts to show signs of pain. "I can hear muffled sounds around me, but I can't make anything out. Even within my own mind I feel groggy and confused all the time. It's not like when I'm here with you, I can't even control myself within my psychological dungeon." They take a deep breath and reach out to hold my hand. "Now that I know that I'll get to see you once a week, I'm going to do whatever I can to keep going. I don't really know how someone keeps their soul from giving up, but I'll sure as hell keep fighting while I'm in this mental prison." He's working so hard to hold it together, it kills me. I scoot to get closer to him and bring his hand up to my lips, I kiss it as tenderly as I can. That simple act makes me feel butterflies in my stomach.

When I look up, he's watching me intently. He licks his lips and starts to lean forward. I bite my bottom lip and hold my breath, eagerly awaiting something I've been dreaming of since the moment I met him— a dream that's only grown since tasting his lips on that rooftop. As we move towards each other, my breathing intensifies. I can smell his skin and I wish I could just stay here with him forever.

The moment our lips touch, my entire body tingles. Instead of getting hot, my body feels like it's freezing from the inside out; it's invigorating. I bite his bottom lip and pull, coaxing out a soft moan. Madís pushes against me with more vigor, his tongue skillfully stroking mine before gently caressing the roof of my mouth. I put my hands on his shoulders and slowly push his body to the ground, straddling his hips. I start to kiss them deeply and with so much hunger, inhaling his scent and enjoying every bit of how he tastes. He wants me just as badly, as his hands start pressing into my shoulder blades and work their way down to the small of my back, then they greedily squeeze my ass as he presses his pelvis into mine.

176

Beep! Beep! Beep! "Shit!" I look up and let go; it's all gone in an instant and I'm back in the compound basement, pulling away from their sweet neck. I step back, keeping my breathing in check, eyes trained forward as I've done so many times before. He's led out with the rest of the humans, and I wish I could at least hold their hand one last time. The heat from their hands pressing against my body still lingers and my entire body is tingling as I long for their touch.

I file out and head straight to my room. My mind is once again heavy after the mind control and as I walk to my dresser I strain to keep my eyes open, I need to take the medication, I already feel horrible. Metztli's right behind me, not wanting me alone when I take it for the first time. I go to the bathroom, pull out 10mg with the provided syringe, and squirt it into my mouth. I look in the mirror and see my pupils dilate briefly before returning to normal. Instantly, I get this huge surge of energy and then I feel like myself again. *That was weird, but not too bad.* I tell Metztli exactly what happened, then crawl into bed and go to sleep, hoping I don't wake up with extra limbs or something.

Chapter 26

The next morning I wake up a little more tired than usual, but otherwise I feel pretty normal. I take one more dose of the medication and head to training. Whatever that shit is, it really works; I feel good, and I'm able to train like always. I stay behind and do 1.5 extra hours then I head to the library. All day today, I've been developing a plan that puts Madís' suggestions into action.

I walk in and confidently walk up to Tomás, who smiles when he sees me. "Hello Superstar, what can I do for you?" I roll my eyes without thinking, then regain my composure; I feel so awkward when I get extra attention. "No need for formalities here, my sweet, this is a safe space. Once you enter these doors, feel free to be who you'd like. There are actually no cameras in here." He gestures to the whole room and then looks back at me and winks. His energy feels like a warm hug from an old friend, I love being near it. The room is so huge I had never noticed it didn't have any cameras.

"Sorry, I'm not used to being complimented. I did want to ask you something—do they have the compound's architectural plans in here?" As I say this he raises his right eyebrow, and cocks his head. Shit, he's suspicious. *Act cool, act cool.* "I've been wanting to review security protocols and I have some concerns about our ability to exit the compound during an emergency. My training here has been fantastic, but they've never gone over escape routes, and that worries me." I say all of this as if my biggest worry is the safety of my fellow Commissioners and I keep the rigid formality I've always displayed.

He puts his hand under his chin and smirks. "Eager little beaver, aren't you? Those records are in our classified section, which you need a special clearance to access. Would you like to apply?"

"Yes, please," I answer, trying hard to hide how important this really is to me. He opens one of the desk drawers, looks through some files and pulls out a packet of papers.

"Fill these out and bring them to me when you're done."

I walk to one of the big wooden tables and get to work. It's all standard information and contracts, swearing me to secrecy, letting me know what will happen if I leak info, *yada, yada.* As I'm doing this I feel strange, as if a shadow has crept into my thoughts. I look at Tomás but he's busy reading his book. I scan the library and quickly ascertain that there is no one else in there. I start to wonder if the medication could be doing this to me before brushing the thought aside, deciding I don't have time to worry about it right now. I quickly complete the packet and bring it back to Tomás.

He takes it without looking away from me. "You are very interesting; Ms. V. I cannot say I have come in contact with a vampire like yourself before. I hope you visit me more; I'd like to get to know you better." A conspiratorial, playful smile spreads across his face; I feel like he's trying to tell me something, but I can't quite grasp it. "This request is seldom made by a cadet; I am going to add a letter in here letting the commission know that I recommended you review these plans in order to continue expand your training."

"But...that's not-"

Tomás shakes his head indicating for me to say no more and smiles, I comply and trust that he knows what he's doing. When I'm near him I feel at home, loved...

Beep…Beep! Beep…Beep! Shit, I wish I could stay and talk to him longer.

"Oh no, I need to go but thank you." I reach out and give his hand a small squeeze.

"Any time my dear, you always know where to find me." He bows his head and I feel as if he's pledging allegiance to me.

As I'm walking I can't stop thinking about Tomás. From the moment I met him I knew there was something more there. I'd been so consumed with training and Madís I had completely forgotten about it. His energy is like a word I can't quite grasp. It's familiar, and right on the tip of my tongue, but no matter how hard I try to figure it out it won't come to me.

When I get to my room Metztli is already sleeping. I get ready as quietly as I can, then slip into a deep sleep as soon as I'm in bed. I wake up easily the next night and get ready for another day of training. Gunny Sophia delivers a kick ass Muay Thai lesson, which I eagerly take in. Once the training is done, we get ready and feed as usual. As we're walking out of the basement I let Metztli know that I'm heading to the library. They nod and join their group mates while I head off on my own.

I walk into the library hoping my request has been granted, and simultaneously eager to see Tomás, I've missed his energy. As I'm walking up to the desk Tomás' eyes twinkle. "Superstar! I've been hoping you'd stop by to see me today."

I smile shyly; something about him makes me feel so comfortable. I wasn't close to my dad growing up and when I'm near Tomás my heart is filled with the fatherly affection I always craved. I never thought someone so connected within this institution would have this kind of energy. "Sir, have you received word about my application?"

"Now, now, no need for formalities here, please, always call me Tomás. Unfortunately, They have not gotten back to me yet, but don't take it personally." At the sound of this I drop my guard and slump my shoulders in disappointment. "These things usually take time. After all, The Commission has not lasted this long without looking at every angle, in every situation very carefully *minha querida*[16]. I do want to show you something; follow me." *Awwww, I love that he just spoke to me in portuguese, what a sweet term.*

He guides me to the second floor of the library and goes to the back corner. There is a section of books that range from ancient to fairly new. "These novels are a pet project of mine. A hundred years ago we had quite a few vampires succumbing to the confinement sickness, and that fancy medication they have now hadn't been invented. I came up with an idea that I proposed to The Commission: these vampires needed an outlet, a way to express their greatest fears and desires, and to imagine the world they'd left behind." He's scanning the shelves as he continues to speak. "I asked if vampires that were struggling could be brought to me, and if I could use writing as a form of therapy. They thought I was a strange old coot, but they will never forget what I did for this institution, so they didn't see the harm in letting me do this. I worked with hundreds of vampires and many of them wrote complete novels." As he speaks, he slides each spine out so it protrudes a little farther than the rest, one with a red spine, one dark blue, and one light purple.

---

[16] My dear; in Portuguese

I've been following his story, but I'm confused. *Why is he sharing this with me? Depressed vampires, novels, what does this have to do with my paperwork?*

"I can see you have no idea where I'm going with this, but I will get to the point soon. Some vampires wrote about their troubles here, their desperation, their need to escape." He lightly taps the spine of each of the books that he's pulled as he says this. "I have pulled the three novels that I feel you will find most interesting. These vampires were surprisingly high up in the organization and their descriptions are vivid. I get a sense that you are an avid reader and would enjoy these novels, *doce menina*[17]." After these last words, he starts to walk away.

I stand there dumbfounded. I take the three books from the shelves and hold them up against my chest. I tilt my head up, close my eyes and whisper, "Thank you."

I walk up to the desk with the books. As Tomás takes them he says, "You are very welcome." He hands them back to me and continues to read his book. I walk out of there in a daze. *What is that man's deal?* I mean don't get me wrong I like it, but I am so thrown off right now, I have no idea what to expect next. As I walk into the room the final curfew bell rings. I sigh, realizing I won't have time to read tonight. I have a feeling that if I start the books now, I'll lose track of time and will risk being overtired at training and that might ultimately rouse suspicions. I leave the books on my desk and start to get ready for bed. Metztli comes in and checks in while they also get ready. "How'd it go in the library, any news?"

---

[17] Sweet girl; in Portuguese

"Nothing from The Commission, but something weird did happen." I explain everything that I experienced with Tomás and all the feelings I've had about him since I first met him.

They're listening to every word excitedly. "I've always known he's chill but I never expected him to be so sneaky, and willing to help you! Ancient guy knows what's up!"

"Yeah, my head's spinning. Tomorrow after my extra training I'll be here reading. I hope these books are as helpful as he made it seem." As we both continue getting ready for bed my hands start to shake suddenly. "Metzli, something's wrong."

They rush over to me and take my hands in theirs; not only are my hands shaking, but they're frozen. I can't move my fingers and my thumbs have tucked into my palm and won't open. We both stand there looking at them, unable to do anything. They hold my hands in theirs and gently massage them. While it doesn't help physically, the motion does calm the anxiety that's growing. Suddenly I collapse, I've also lost all sensation in my legs, and my weight gives out underneath me. I could stand if I needed to but they feel as if they're asleep. After twenty minutes my hands finally stop shaking, the tension releases, and I slowly regain feeling and control over my fingers. The blood begins to rush into my legs and the tingling slowly subsides.

Metzli sits with me the entire time. They caress my arms, help me breathe deeply, and try to take my mind off of what's happening. Once it's over we sit on the edge of my bed. I'm so freaked out right now, I want to scream, cry, rip something up. Metzli puts their hands on my shoulders and turns my body so that we're facing each other. They put their lips to my forehead and then don't move. I close my eyes and lean into them, I let their energy flow over and into me. We sit like this for a long time, and once I'm ready to talk I start to pull away.

While we're still facing each other Metzli asks, "V, has that ever happened to you before?" I can tell they're terrified but they're trying so hard to stay calm for me.

"My hands shake when I'm anxious, but I wasn't nervous at all right now. It's also never been that bad. This must be a result of the medication." I look down at my hands and turn them, examining every crease, as if what I just experienced could have changed them in some way.

"I thought the doctor said you wouldn't have any side effects," they say, confused.

"He did, but I got a bad feeling from him, definitely not the kind of person I can trust. This honestly doesn't surprise me—I kept waiting for side effects. But you know I'm not going to stop taking it." My voice starts to get defensive as I fear that Metzli won't let me continue using it after this episode. "I don't care what happens to me as long as I can live long enough to get Madís out." As I say this, I look at Metzli, my face begging them not to take this from me.

"I know. I'll never try to stop you, but I'm glad I can at least be here for you." They give my hands a gentle squeeze and then wrap me in the most comforting hug I've ever experienced. Before releasing them I slowly kiss their cheek and whisper, "Thank you for being so wonderful. I love you".

They turn their head so that we are facing each other and put their forehead against mine. "I love you too, *cihuapohtli*[18]." We both

---

[18] This word literally means "a woman like me" in Nahuatl. It is a term of endearment that signifies a strong bond.

smile and Metzli walks over to their bed. I crawl under my covers and sigh heavily. My life doesn't matter anymore. As long as I can get Madís out, I'll die happy knowing they're safe.

Chapter 27

I wake up the next day feeling normal. No shaking, no other side effects. It sucks that I now know this medication must be doing something to my system, but it's too late to turn back. It's allowing me to do what I need in order to help Madís, and for that I'm grateful.

Training is uneventful and I stay behind as usual to get my individual practice in. I don't even need the extra review anymore, but I know The Commission has come to expect it. If I stop, I feel like they'll think something's up, or they may question my dedication. Part of me being Their superstar isn't just that I'm skilled, it's that it seems as if I'm committed to Their cause. They like that I eat, breathe, and dream about training—at least that's how I've made it seem. I need to make sure They continue to see me in this way, and if that means spending extra time doing something I enjoy anyway, I don't mind.

Once I'm done for the day, I head to my room and go straight to my desk. I open the drawer and pull-out lined paper and a pen from the stock of office supplies provided to each desk. The three books I checked out yesterday are piled one on top of another, and I grab the red one since it's at the top of the pile. I start reading, not knowing what to expect. I was already a fast reader as a human, and as a vamp I read at hyper speed.

This book's a thriller, about a Lieutenant who's seeing things in the darkness of the compound; it's actually pretty good. Right off the bat I start getting descriptions of this place, but at first, it's stuff I've seen and already know about. Halfway through the book I find what I'm looking for. The Lieutenant discloses that there are tunnels connected to room 1B. They were created for a quick escape but are on a need to know basis for those residing in the compound. The curfew bell rings and I've finished the book, but it's left me with a lot to try and figure out.

I get into bed and put my headphones on, hoping that if I listen to certain songs I'll be able to think as I fall asleep. I'm wired and my mind's racing. As I listen to "Bullet with Butterfly Wings" by **The Smashing Pumpkins** a plan slowly starts to form in my mind. *I may not be as bad at this as I thought.*

The next few days I continue my usual routine, but every day after training or feeding I come to my room to plan. I decided I don't want to write anything down, since there can't be any evidence of what I'm doing. I bounce ideas off of Metztli, who finds holes in everything I come up with in the beginning. Instead of getting frustrated, I'm grateful for their feedback, because my plan needs to be solid.

The first thing I figure out is how I'll get down to room 1B. On feeding days we either take the elevator or the stairs down to room 1A. When you enter our feeding area there is a door directly across from the entrance where the donors enter. I've always been able to get a glimpse of stairs leading downward as they walk in. Those stairs lead down to floor 1B. Without the proper clearance I'd be detected immediately if I tried using that staircase, so I'm going to ask Lieutenant Angelo if I can volunteer with the donors. I'm really pushing my luck but getting out of here is going to require bold moves.

Tonight, I'm jittery as hell. I get to feed off Madís and the thought of them consumes me. Metztli knows I've been counting down the days until I see them, and before we leave they give my hand a little squeeze. We walk out the door and head to the basement. By now the routine has become standard, and even though my mouth still waters the moment I smell them, I know I'll have what I've been craving soon enough.

As I sink my fangs into their neck I take a second to enjoy the taste of them; *es el sabor de mi hogar,*[19] the rich flavors of our *cultura*[20] flowing out of them. It takes everything in me not to moan. Without consciously trying, I transport us to a bedroom. As soon as their mind clears they look around and smile. We're in a luxury apartment at night, the glowing L.A. skyline framed by a huge window. There's a king sized bed in the middle with white sheets, surrounded by black walls, and candles on practically every surface.

"You get right to the point, don't you?" They ask with a smirk on their face.

"Subtlety has never been my strong suit. I know what I want, why not just go for it?" As I say this I'm crawling on the bed over to them. Suddenly, I realize that I do have info to share before I get caught up in all of this. My autistic brain will not be able to get in the mood if I don't take care of business first. I sit up on my knees. "Oh shoot, before we go too far I do need to tell you that your suggestions last week really helped, and I am in the middle of a plan."

As scared as they are, I can see hope in their eyes. "I knew you'd figure out a way," Madís whispers as they kneel in front of me and start to kiss my neck. They begin gently at first, but as they take in my taste and scent, they want more, lifting my black shirt and pulling off my sports bra. Baby Boy pushes me down on the bed and drags his tongue from my collar bone down in between my breasts. My eyes are

---

[19] It's the flavor of my home; in Spanish
[20] Culture; in Spanish

closed and I'm moaning with ecstasy, while my hands rake through his hair.

I bring them up to me and whisper, "Can I bite you?" They nod and we switch places. I look deeply into their eyes first and, without thinking, I start playing "If Only" by **Hollywood Principle and Al3jandro** in the background. I lick their perfect heart shaped lips, gently nibble their jaw, and kiss my way down to their neck right above their collarbone. As I sink my fangs in, they let out a deep moan and grab my inner thighs, squeezing as I suck. Their taste is more than the usual richness of blood...*it's life, it's our people's existence, its fresh earth, and gentle rain.* I can see the entire universe and Madís and I are the only ones in it, our bodies becoming one.

As I release them I lick the puncture wounds to stop their blood from trickling down. I lay next to them on my side and they face me, panting, working their index finger from my shoulder down to my nipple. They look at me and say, "How did you do that? You made me orgasm without touching me. All you did was feed."

I laugh. "There's a lot more to connection than sex Baby Boy, I've found that I can have a deeper experience with someone when I feed than any other way. I will happily go down on you next time though, your taste is irresistible. Remember, I have access to all of your fantasies when your blood flows through me." While I talk, I brush their bangs aside, which had gotten mussed from my fingers and their sweat. "Our time is almost up," I say sadly.

"I know." He pulls me close, and we hold each other until I hear the beep.

Once again, they file out with the rest of the humans, and I return to my room–that dreadful routine that I've come to despise.

When I'm not near him I feel like a part of me is missing, like my heart is no longer whole. I've always been one to turn my pain into motivation, so I use this emptiness to continue to fuel me, and to remind me of why I can't fail.

Chapter 28

After training the next day I head straight to Lieutenant Angelo's office. When I walk in, he motions for me to sit. Although I've only visited this room a few times it's become quite familiar, nothing ever changes. The same metal chair that I always sit in is there, a metal desk with paper, and folders organized perfectly. The computer is always on, and I've never dared to try and glance at the screen, but I have always wondered what he works on all day.

"How have you been, Cadet V? You had us quite worried with your confinement sickness. We don't want anything to happen to our most promising cadet."

"Thank you for your concern, Lieutenant. With the doctor's help I am doing very well." I answer with complete admiration for the Vamp Doc coming through in my voice.

"That is good to hear, he is quite skilled. I see you have been keeping up with your studies and your instructors continue to report impressive progress." He looks like a proud dad at their kid's awards assembly. I know he's getting a lot of credit and recognition for being my Lieutenant. I'm working hard not to let our last interaction change the way I behave towards him. From the moment I walked into the room I've had a huge lump in my throat.

"Sir, I am here today because I have decided that I would like to stay with The Commission past my ten-year obligation. I have finally found my place in the world and it's here, with this organization." I've kept my formal composure as it's what he's come to expect from me.

He's sitting up and his eyes are full of excitement. "This is wonderful news, cadet, wonderful news indeed! The Commission was hoping you'd come to this decision."

I continue, "I know that I am not like the other cadets; they are all skilled, but they do not possess the passion that I do. I would like to request further training and I would like to volunteer throughout the compound. I plan on perhaps spending eternity serving The Commission and I'm hungry for more involvement. I'm willing to start my volunteer hours right away, perhaps with the donors. The system you have here is exemplary and I'd like to learn more."

He's been nodding as I've been speaking and thinking carefully about everything I'm suggesting. "I have noticed that you do not interact with the other cadets, I can see how your need to train beyond what is expected would make it difficult for you to connect with them." He is standing behind his desk and pacing as he considers what I've said. "I have also noticed that you seem bored, restless... What you are requesting would require you to receive quite a bit of clearance." He quickly sits at his desk and starts to type and analyze information on his screen.

I don't dare ask what he's doing, I sit as still as a statue and wait for his response. After several minutes he speaks again. "I see here that you did submit paperwork to view the compound blueprints, but that process will take quite a while. It bodes well for you that Tomás included a letter of recommendation, and that he was the one to suggest you increase your knowledge here. That man is a genius, this institution would not be what it is today if it was not for him." He's still looking at his screen as he speaks, the glow of the monitor glistening off his smooth head.

"I am going to speak to my superior about this and I will get back to you." He's looked away from the computer screen and is now smiling at me. "I must say I have never had the pleasure of working with such a dedicated recruit. You are destined for great things, Cadet V."

"Thank you, Sir. None of it would be possible without your constant guidance. I am very fortunate that I was assigned to your unit." As I say this, a twinge of guilt hits me; I'm planning on betraying the Lieutenant and everything he holds dear. He's not a bad person, even after the last incident. He just believes in this institution's mission more than anything and is willing to do whatever it takes to protect it. It's the same way I feel about Madís, and those that I love. We each have our passions, interests, and loyalties that guide and consume us.

I know that when I execute my plan the Lieutenant will be heavily scrutinized for trusting me, and giving me so much power, but there's no other way. As I'm thinking all of this I'm standing, bowing, and walking out the door. No matter what I do, I'm hurting someone. I need to find comfort in the fact that I'm saving the most innocent player in this game.

I go to my room and head straight for my desk. I want to read the next book Tomás suggested, anticipating that it will give me more information about the compound. The more I know about this place, the better; I don't want any surprises.

In the next few days, my expectations are exceeded by the other two novels. I memorize an incredible amount of information about the security system. Tomás must be the only other vamp that has ever read these books, there's no way The Commission would knowingly display Their tightly kept secrets in the library. *Why didn't he report this? And why is he trusting me with them?*

Three days after I meet with Lieutenant Angelo, a Commissioner comes to me after practice and tells me that after feeding today I will follow the officer that escorts the donors in order to start my volunteering. I repress my smile, keeping my composure and nodding my head. *It's happening! I'm pulling this off!*

Feeding goes as usual and, once I'm done, I step out of line and stand behind the officer that escorted the humans in. The prefects and cadets are staring at me while staying at attention. Out of the corner of my eye I see Erik sneer for a second and then regain his composure immediately. The other cadette's emit confusion and resentment. *Fuckin Erik, get over it.* I've gotten used to it by now, and there are more important matters at hand than the other cadetes' view of me.

I follow the officer down the hallway to a staircase that leads us farther down, the humans following our every move. The stairwell is made of old brick and the stairs are metal, the donors' footsteps make a clanging echo as they step. We get to a door and the officer scans his badge to unlock it.

As I walk in, I have to contain my shock. I don't know what I was expecting, but I didn't think it was going to be this horrible. The room is full of 9x9 foot cells, each with a metal toilet in the back and one metal chair. The human has just enough room to stand, take a few steps to the toilet or walk around their chair. There are hundreds of these cells lined up in two levels around the perimeter of the room. The bars are made of a thick metal but are painted white, the stairs that lead up to the second level are of the same material. Most humans are sitting, their eyes lost, but some are pacing their small enclosures like mindless zombies. They moan, scream, cry while all of the officers in here ignore them.

We walk up to the platform leading to the second level, and there's a row of empty cells with the doors open. The officer I'm with walks the humans to the first cell, and files our group in one-by-one. As each one walks in he closes the door and it locks behind them. Each door has a keypad that needs to be unlocked by a card. I'm studying every aspect of the room and every device used to keep it secure. There are cameras every few feet, high up against the walls. There are no blind spots anywhere with how much surveillance is in here.

Once all of the humans are in their cells, the officer takes me to the bottom floor and starts explaining the whole operation. As I'm walking, the acid in my stomach turns. The smell is overpowering, it's like rancid meat left in the heat, *do these other vamps really not notice?* The humans are bathed and changed every three days, they get taken out for two hours every night except for when it's their donor day (the day we feed from them), and they're fed three meals a day, with water at each meal.

As he's talking, my mouth waters, letting me know that Madís is near; I listen intently but start to scan out of my peripherals and then I see him. He's sitting in cell 227, devoid of everything that makes him magical, practically a ghost. I continue walking and force myself not to bat an eye. As we walk farther down I see a large grey metal door tucked into the far left corner of the building, it has a small black keypad right below the elongated doorknob. This place is under such strict security; I have no idea how I'm going to get past any of it. My mind's spinning but I've got to keep my cool on the outside.

After the tour, the officer tells me that I'll usually be here around mealtime so I'll help distribute food trays, and then collect them. He walks me to an elevator and presses the 1C button, then we descend, and the doors open to a huge room with different doorways. This hallway looks like all the others in the compound: grey walls, grey doors, grey concrete floors. He explains that one contains showers, one stores all of the donor's scrubs, one is a medical facility/extermination center, and the one we're going to is the kitchen.

We walk in and it looks more like a factory than a kitchen. There's a black conveyor belt that's constantly being fed with tan plastic trays; as they move down the line, a row of metal tubes squeeze mush into compartments, distinguishable only by slight variations in color. It looks disgusting but I guess the humans don't care since they're not conscious anyway. At the end of the conveyor is a huge metal rolling rack, where an officer is stacking the trays at lightning speed. Once the rack is full, that officer pushes it towards the door, and another officer takes their place.

"This process is straightforward. You're going to be filling your shelves, and when you head to 1B the officer at the door will direct you to the next set of donors that need to be fed. Your key card has already been given clearance for all of our locks. You will unlock the cell, place the tray on the donor's lap, close the door and move onto the next. When your racks are empty, come back here to fill them up again." I'm listening and nodding as he gestures to the conveyor belt and racks. "By the time the conveyor is done, it will be time to start collecting the trays. You'll go to 1B with your empty shelves and just do the job in reverse. When you get down here you'll put the trays on the conveyor belt and it will go backwards to collect and wash everything. It's mind-numbing work, but it's easy."

I'm showing this officer an extreme amount of respect as I listen to his instructions. I've heard that being assigned to donor care is the lowest Commission job possible. The commissioners who are here couldn't make it on missions and end up doing the grunt work. I know what it feels like to be treated like you aren't good enough, and although I hate this system, I want this officer to feel that I respect him just as much as my Lieutenant.

He walks me to an empty rack, and I get in line with the other officers that are waiting to fill theirs. I file in and get to work. I have to turn everything off inside of me so that my anxiety doesn't take over, it hurts so much to see them like this. Even the scent of the humans rips my heart apart-they smell as if they're decaying even though they're still fully alive. I don't know if other vamps pick up on this, or if it's just because of my sensory processing disorder, but it makes my stomach turn.

This place shouldn't exist. *We shouldn't exist.* I wish I could get them all out of here, but even then there are thousands of these compounds around the world. What about those humans? I have to live with the fact that Madís is the only one I can save, and I honestly don't even know if I'll be able to pull that off.

Once their feeding's over, it's time for me to head to bed. I learn that during the day there are two guards that are awake so that the humans are always guarded. I'll continue to learn how everything runs as I volunteer, but Madís is running out of time.

I crawl into bed and am so disappointed in myself, repulsed by what I've just taken part in and the system I'm helping to uphold. I put on my headphones because music is the only way I'll be able to shut all of this out. As "Hello Operator" by **The White Stripes** comes on, I recall the smell of the humans' rotting souls and gag quietly. Eventually the beat consumes me, and I drift off to sleep.

Chapter 29

I'm told that I'll be volunteering underground two days a week, this doesn't console me though because time is ticking and Madís' extermination date isn't too far off. Something tells me I should go talk to Tomás, that he may be the key to unlocking this whole thing. His gentle hazel eyes flash into my memory. *Why do you always hold back, as much as your energy calls to me I know you're hiding something.*

After my extra training, I head straight to the library. When I walk in I listen to see if anyone else is in there, and I'm relieved that he and I are the only ones there. He perks up in his chair and gives me his usual greeting. "Superstar! Long time no see, I've been wondering what you've been up to. Of course, I do hear all of the whispers around the compound, and know that you are quite the busy bee, but I always prefer to hear it from the source." He gives me a wink and a sweet smile as he says this.

It's hard for me to drop the formality I've gotten so used to using in this place, even though I do feel comfortable around him, "Yes Sir...I mean Tomás, I have thoroughly enjoyed the books you recommended. They were exactly what I was looking for." I slide the books across his desk. I look behind me quickly and then say, "I get the feeling you have the answer to something..." He holds his hand up and then puts his finger to his lips.

"I am excited to announce that you received the clearance to view the compound's blueprints," he's speaking formally, it's so out of character for him I squirm out of discomfort.

"It's okay, I don't..." he once again holds his hand up and slowly shakes his head no.

"If you follow me I can show you how to access the files." He gets up and starts walking to the back right corner of the library. He reaches under one of the shelves and I hear a click as the shelf pops open and reveals a metal door. He scans his key card, and the door unlocks. We walk into a room with metal walls, bare except for a metal desk, a chair, and a computer.

Once we're inside he closes the door behind him and starts speaking quickly. "I know you don't need the plans anymore. This is the only room that is so enforced that no vampire anywhere in this facility can hear us speak. From this day forward your key card has been activated to access this room." He's standing close to me and although he said no one would be able to hear us here, he's whispering.

"I know you are planning an escape. I've seen it attempted many, many times. I know I cannot talk you out of it, and a fire like yours should not be kept in a place like this. I am willing to help in any way I can, and I want you to know that you have an ally in me."

I stand there stunned; this is not what I was expecting at all. I can sense he's being sincere. "Tomás, I thank you with all my heart, but this isn't about me. There's a human that I need to get out of here, one who holds my entire soul. I don't care if I make it out of here, but I need to make sure that they do."

As I say this Tomás closes his eyes, a pained look appearing across his face as he slowly nods. "I understand more than you could ever imagine, *menina*. There is something we cannot shake about our humanity. Yes, they are our food source, but some of us never lose touch with what we used to be." A deep sadness emanates from within him and wraps itself around me. "We're drawn to it, and the frailty that humans exude is somewhat irresistible to us. As hard as it is to deal with this constant battle within us it keeps us from ever fully giving into the darkness that our species inherits. I will do whatever you need me to." He bows with his arms outstretched and palms facing up, it's such a sweet, antiquated gesture my eyes start to water.

"I don't know what to say, thank you doesn't seem like enough."

"No need to thank me; I have my own reasons for wanting you out of here as well, I do not have time to explain now, but I promise it will be revealed to you when the time is right. I have sensed that once you get out of the facility you have no way of getting away from here." They narrow their eyes and stare right into mine.

I look at the floor and nod because he's right, I haven't been able to figure this part out, and I kept hoping something would come to me.

"The day before you plan on escaping, hold my image in your mind, I will take care of the rest. There will be someone ready for you when you are out of the compound."

I look up, stunned. "What do you—"

"There's no time to elaborate, I have already been here far too long. I need you to trust me. Can you do that?"

I look deep into his eyes and my instinct whispers yes. I nod.

"Wonderful. I must go back out in case anyone walks in. You can stay and look at the files if you'd like. Trust in yourself my dear, there is so much more to you than most realize." He suddenly turns and quickly exits the room.

I stand there in a daze, *what just happened?* I'm running through the entire conversation in my head, replaying everything that Tomás just said. My brain is too overloaded right now and I need to get back to my room to process everything. As I walk out I see that Tomás is at his desk, reading a book and acting completely casual. I nod at him on my way out and hold my controlled demeanor.

I head straight to my room and am glad that Metztli is there already. Shit, I can't tell them what I found and risk anyone else hearing everything that I've discovered. Today's interaction with Tomás made me realize how careless we've been, talking about all of this when anyone could be outside our room, or in the hallway.

When I walk into the room, I see that they're sitting against their headboard reading. Their boots are neatly lined next to the foot of their bed, and they've changed into their pajamas- the standard grey sweats and white t-shirt that we all get. I go up to their right ear and whisper, "I have an idea, but I need you to trust me." Metztli's nervous but they have faith in me, so they nod and turn to face me. I kneel next to their bed and reach up. I put my hands on either side of their jaw and look straight into their eyes. I concentrate and try to reach into their mind, try to access their soul. I start to work through the fog until I'm in a black room with Metztli, who looks around, dazed.

"Where are we? What did you do?" they stammer, thrown off guard.

"We're in your mind. As I was walking to our room today it came to me that I'd never tried to enter a vampire's mind while drinking fresh human blood. My powers have never been at full capacity. Now that I'm drinking as often as I am, straight from the source, my gift is much stronger than I could ever imagine. If I concentrate hard enough, I can do this to anyone."

"Holy shit, V, this is next level," they exclaim, in awe.

"I know. We shouldn't be here for too long, though, so I need to tell you everything that's just happened." I run through my interaction with Tomás and everything that I learned as they stare at me, eyes wide. As soon as I'm done, I pull us out and we're back in our room. I go to the bathroom and take another 10 mg of my medication because I have no idea what vamp mind control will do to me, and I don't want to find out.

All of a sudden, a sharp pain sears into my brain. I fight the urge to scream as I crouch down on the floor, grasping my head, trying to hold it together. It's as if my skull's being torn apart, and I wonder if my head's going to explode, who knows what this shit is doing to my body. Metztli runs in and puts their arms around me, knowing there's nothing else they can do. After a few seconds, the pain subsides and I'm able to stand up straight. When I look at them I can see it all on their face—how worried they are about me, how much they hate that I take the medication, and the utter helplessness that they feel.

"I can't stop, and you know that," I reply to their unspoken concerns, before turning and walking to my bed.

We both lay down, but the mood in the room remains heavy. There's nothing I can say or do to make things better, so I leave things as they are and go to sleep.

Chapter 30

I continue with my new routine each day–train, volunteer some days, whatever it takes to prepare until the next time I get to feed from Madís. My plan is coming together, and I feel like I can execute it as soon as a couple of weeks. Everyone on the donor floor trusts me, and I've even been asked to fill in for some of the daytime workers. On those days I'm excused from training and get to sleep for two days. I'm so ahead of the other recruits that missing training doesn't affect me. This level of trust and responsibility is what will allow me to implement my plan.

Today is finally my special feeding day, and I'm so anxious that I can barely contain my stimming. I've been playing music in my head all day, and going extra hard in training, to the point that I almost dislocated my partner's arm because I was concentrating so hard. As soon as I can, I head to room 1B and line up in front. Madís walks out looking more worn than the last time I saw them; I don't know how much longer they will last here.

I sink my teeth into their shoulder and take a minute to inhale their scent. Even with the stagnant smell of what this place is doing to them, I can still pick up a hint of their earthy essence. This time I transport us to *Shine*, the club where we met. The music is blaring but we're the only two in there; even the DJ booth is empty. They run up to me and we embrace.

"I miss you so much." I whisper as they hug me even tighter. "Sweet one, I've finally figured out how to get you out of here," I lean in and kiss them with everything that's inside of me–all of the fear, love, pain, every emotion I've been holding onto turns into unbridled passion. As we're kissing, tears start to roll down my cheeks because I want them to be safe more than anything, more than my desire for them, more than my own safety. I've finally found what makes me want to live, and it's them.

We sit cross legged in front of each other and I go through my entire plan. They're listening to every word, hope building as they start to really believe that I'm going to pull this off. As I'm talking, I look at them sadly because they have no idea that I don't plan on making it out of here alive; it will be daytime when I want to get them out of here, so when we make it to the surface I'll either disintegrate or I'll stay in the tunnels and get caught. I haven't decided which I'd prefer, but I'm sure once the moment arrives, I'll know what to do.

If this is the last time I get to be with them I'm going to make it count. I dim the lights in the club and turn on the colored strobes. The mood changes immediately and I start playing "Una Vaina Loca" by **Fuego, Manuel Turizo,** and **Duki.** The small dingy club has now turned into our magical oasis. While I hold their hands, I make a figure eight with my hips as I seductively move to standing. They arch their back as they follow my lead, their face tracing the front of my body, from my ankles up to my face. Moving to the beat together, I turn around and wrap their arms around my waist. Their lips are at my neck and I'm pressing against them, the rhythm filling our souls and tying us together, just like the first time we danced. *"Siempre acuérdate de este momento, mi angel,[21]"* I whisper as I close my eyes and sway with them, letting their heartbeat and the rhythm guide me, wishing this moment would last forever.

---

[21] Always remember this moment my angel; said in Spanish

They bite my earlobe, causing me to gasp with delight, before replying, "I don't regret any of this, it brought me to you *mi reina*.[22] I'd do it all over again as long as I'd still get to have these moments with you."

Beep! Beep! Beep! I turn, slowly kiss their collar bone, and we disappear one last time.

I'm back in the basement, the humans are filing out and I'm heading to my room in a daze. I take my medication, crawl into bed, and continue to plan our escape. I ignore the fact that my head is pounding, my heart's racing, and the medication feels like lead in my stomach.

Later that week I receive communication that I will be filling in for a day officer in two days. They give me fair warning because I will have to change my sleep patterns and plan to miss my usual activities. This is it; I'm getting Madís out. I know I had promised to tell Metztli once it was time, but I decided a while ago that once I was going to actually escape, I wasn't going to say anything. Once They figure out what I've done, they will be the first to get questioned, and if I keep them in the dark then maybe they stand a chance of getting out of this alive. Metzli is going to be so angry at me, but they'll understand why I did what I did, and know that I was driven by my love for them. They've supported me through all of this, and the last thing I want is for them to be punished because of my actions.

I also hold Tomás' imagine in my mind, just as he asked me to, and hope that I'm doing this correctly.

---

[22] My queen; in Spanish

Chapter 31

The day I'm set to volunteer, I place my medication in my pants pocket. *Who knows, it may come in handy.* I walk over to Metztli, who's peacefully sleeping, and I gently kiss their cheek. *"Gracias por todo amor.²³"* I walk out without looking back, hoping that my actions don't hurt them too much.

I scan my badge and head into room 1B, ready to roll out the plan. After checking in with the guard I'm relieved, I walk to every cell to make sure that the humans don't need anything. I check the first floor and then go up to the top, I nod at the Commissioner who's stationed up there. Then I take my place at the guard post on the lower level and stand at attention, not moving an inch for the next few hours.

Enough time has passed to warrant another walk through. Just as before, I stroll along the room's perimeter, giving each cell a cursory check. Once I reach Madís, however, I pause, peering in closely. They look like a walking cadaver, with sunken-in, almost hollow looking eyes, and sickly yellow skin. They're still under complete compulsion and they stare at the bars as they sit and sway slightly. I have to fight back my tears and extreme rage; *I need to stay in control.* After taking it all in I jog to the upper platform.

"Hey, the donor in cell 227 is acting weird, I think something's wrong with them. I'm going to log it into the computer and then walk them to the medical facility." The officer looks at me and nods; other members of Madís' group have started to die and it's not unusual for a

---

²³ Thanks for everything love; in Spanish

few to be taken to the facility each day. He stays at attention as I walk back down.

I walk to the computer, pretending to type up an incident report, but instead I quickly key in the codes that I've memorized. I'm able to turn off the cameras in this room, and in the tunnels leading out of here. I'm also able to upload the virus I learned about in the book to make it harder to detect the shut-off, and to prolong the control panel from getting the cameras back up. All of this works perfectly, the info in those books is legit.

I jog to Madís' cell; whenever we take someone to the medical facility we try to be quick so that the other guard isn't left alone for long, since it's a lot to watch over. Knowing that my haste won't seem unusual, I unlock the door at lightning speed.

"Ugh, gross, I hate touching them when they're like this," I purposefully mutter. All of a sudden I hear a human in the upper level start to vomit, followed by the footfalls of the officer running over to inspect them. I'll be expected to take them to the medical facility, too. *Shit, I need to hurry.*

I stealthily sneak us over to the metal door at the far end of the room. I scan my badge and slip into the tunnel that was described in the books Tomás gave me. I throw Madís over my shoulder and start running through the tunnel as fast as possible. They're completely limp, a rag doll that I've wrapped my arms around. I'm making good speed, but I can make out the sounds above. Numerous footsteps in the upper levels indicate that the guard has alerted the control center that Madís and I have gone missing. I have more working against me than I had anticipated. *Fuck! I was supposed to have more time than this!* As fast as I'm able to move, I don't think I'm going to make it to the end of the tunnel in time.

At the next fork turn left.

What the fuck? Whose voice is that?

Just do as I say.

My adrenaline's so high that I don't have time to try and figure out what's going on. I turn at the next fork. This isn't the path I had planned on taking, but there will be an entire team waiting for me at the exit. *What do I have to lose?*

The tunnel ends at a thick rusted metal ladder.

Climb! Quickly!

With Madís still over my shoulder, I start to ascend, moving faster than I ever have before. I stop when I get to a small square doorway above my head, which easily opens with a light push. The moment I peek my head into the room I realize it's the metal room that Tomás had taken me into the last time we spoke.

I close the latch and gently place Madís on the floor. Only then do I realize that I'm shaking from all of the adrenaline that's rushing through me. I'm not tired or out of breath, but I feel like a trapped animal. We would have never made it out with my original plan, but I have no idea what I'll do while trapped in here. I sit on the floor next to Madís and try to collect my thoughts.

The entire compound is going to be crawling with agents now that they know I've escaped. *Shit, I guess I'm not as good at this as I thought.* I sit there, defeated, seeing no way to pull this off. I stroke Madís' hair but don't dare take them out of their trance. I don't want to tell them that I've failed, that we'll soon be discovered. I'd rather they die while in their prison and never see it coming.

I pull him into my lap and hold his head against my chest. I want at least a few more hours with him before it's all over. After sitting together for two hours, I hear the door unlock. I brace myself for what's to come, for it all to end. The door swings open, and I see Tomás. To my relief, he's alone! He walks in swiftly and shuts the door behind him. He's holding a plastic bag and a large glass jar full of water.

He hands them to me as he's speaking, "I was hoping you were receiving my messages, Superstar. From the moment I saw you I knew you had The Gift. You've put this place in quite the uproar. It's like you've disappeared into thin air, and they don't know what to do with themselves.

"Lucky for you, vampires are quite impatient. They will search for you today and then move onto the outer perimeter and beyond. I have a plan to get you out of here, just sit tight. FYI, your key card has been disabled. That's why I left the secret doorway unlocked. Remember, no matter how good your plan is, it's always prudent to have a plan B. Oh! And those items are for your human to stay hydrated and relieve themselves."

He's about to unlock the door when I'm suddenly gripped with terror. "Wait! Tomás, if they're tearing this place apart looking for me, won't they find the ladder? The secret door?" I'm starting to freak out as I ask this, my anxiety spiraling.

"*Menina*, you really must give me more credit. Do you think I've lasted this long by ignoring such things? I am more powerful than you can imagine, my dear. I am able to make ANYONE see, feel, and experience what I want them to. When they search the tunnels all they will find when they get to the ladder is a dead end..." his voice trails off, a look of tenderness on his face. "I really did hope we would get more time together, there is so much I would like to teach you about The Gift. But maybe someday I will still get the chance."

Speechless, I walk over and embrace him in a long hug. His scent is of incense and strength, such an amazing soul. He doesn't wait for my response before he rushes to the door and slides out.

I sit there in complete shock, this vamp's an evil genius. He was one step ahead of me the entire time. I wonder how long he's been able to read my thoughts; he was able to communicate with me in the tunnels, but he seemed to know exactly what I was doing long before that. Someone as old as Tomás would have a tremendous amount of power, and there's no telling what kind of other gifts he possesses. Why would someone so powerful choose to live life as a librarian, and to risk it all for me and Madís?

All of this has put me at ease for the first time today. Since it looks like we have a chance at survival, I decide to wake Madís up. I lay them on the ground and look deeply into their eyes. "It's time to wake up, *mi amor,*[24] I say, telepathically. Their eyes flutter and I can see the haze clear. Smiling at me, they reach their hand up and touch my jaw. In response I turn my head and kiss their palm.

"Is this real? Did you get us out?" they ask groggily.

"This is real, baby, but I haven't gotten us out yet. We're in a safe place for now, but we're still in the compound. Things didn't go as well as I planned but we have someone on the inside." As I talk, my eyes tear up because I can't believe I'm here with them in the flesh, and not just some vision in their mind. I help them sit up, and they slowly wrap their arms around my neck. I hold their shaking body against my own, rocking them back and forth as I reach into their mind. *It's okay,*

---

[24] My love; in Spanish

Baby Boy, I'm here with you. We're going to be just fine. We're going to get out of here.

They relax in my arms and I'm in heaven. I bury my face into their hair and breathe them in. "I love you so much."

They look up at me, stunned. "I've never deserved someone like you, my whole life I've been a screw-up, never lived up to anyone's expectations. How on earth can someone as perfect as you love me?"

I smile and answer, "Because you're magic, and I don't want you to ever forget that."

I hand them the items that Tomás brought for them, and they blush. Not super sexy to relieve yourself into a bag with someone you haven't even slept with in the room, but it is what it is.

We hold each other for hours. If I could stay here forever I would. As we sit there in each other's arms I notice how weak and frail they are. Their breathing is labored, and they've lost so much weight I can feel the sharpness of their bones through their clothing. Their body seems to tremor every few minutes and they come in and out of consciousness. *Hold on, angel, I promise I'll get you to safety, if you can just stay strong a little longer.* I keep this part to myself; I don't want them to know how scared I am.

All of a sudden, I hear the door being opened, at first I'm not concerned assuming it's Tomás but as the door creaks, and I can hear sounds from the outside, I realize that he's not alone. *This is it; this is where it all ends, how could I have been stupid enough to think that I'd pull this off?* I repress frightened tears, Madís still sleeping in my lap. I brace myself for the inevitable arrest.

"This is where classified documents are stored. It's small but feel free to look around if you'd like." Tomás is completely calm, his gentle demeanor as normal as ever. *What the hell?*

Two commissioners dressed in the usual black shirt, cargo pants, and boots peer into the small room. It's easy to scan within a few seconds and I hear one say, "The library's clear, moving on." Tomás shuts the door and they're gone just as quickly as they arrived. *Fucking shit, that's right! Tomás can control them!*

After about a day the door opens and Tomás slides in, looking disheveled and grinning widely. I've never seen him like this. "You really did it, Superstar! They've been turning this place upside down looking for you." He notices that Madís has regained consciousness and turns to them, a little calmer. "I'm so sorry for my rudeness. I'm Tomás, it's wonderful to finally meet the person who was able to capture this beautiful creature's heart." He motions to me as he says these last few words. "Excuse the fact that we won't be able to get to know each other better, but time is of the essence. V, it's nighttime and they've now assumed that you are out of the compound. The search has been expanded to the surrounding areas." My face falls and my heart sinks. We'll be hunted for life.

"Now, now, *menina*, you didn't think you'd get out of here and then be off scot-free, did you? You're smarter than that. No need to worry, I have contacts on the outside that are willing to help." He's put his hands on my shoulders and is looking deeply into my eyes. "It is crucial that you make it to them as quickly as possible, they will have to maneuver their vehicle in order to prevent from being captured. If you think The Commission has some fancy gadgets just wait until you see what this group possesses." Tomás' eyes narrow and an almost evil smile spreads across his lips. I've never seen him be anything but warm and cheery, it's like I'm looking at a different person.

The expression dissipates just as quickly as it appeared, and he continues his explanation. *Did I just imagine that? No, he changed...*

There isn't time for me to stress about any of it though and I continue listening, "You will take the ladder that led you to this room back down to the tunnel. Behind it you will notice another tunnel. From there, I want you to take it all the way to the end. It is a very old sewage drain with no cameras, but you must still be as quick as possible. There are ears everywhere and there's no telling who may hear you moving around down there. That sewage system will end at a grate where a car will be waiting to transport you to an undisclosed destination. From there you can plan your next move."

Tomás takes both of my hands into his, brings them up to his lips, and kisses them. "I believe in very few people, Superstar, and I stick my neck out for no one, but you are destined for great things. As soon as I close the door, leave immediately." He quickly unlocks the trapdoor, nods at Madís, and slips out the big metal door.

I pull Madís onto my back, open the trap door, and run down the stairs as quickly and nimbly as possible. I get to the bottom and follow the tunnel Tomás described behind the ladder. Despite wading through water and sludge, I don't slow down. We get to yet another ladder that leads up to a grate. "We're almost there, *mi amor*," I whisper, before climbing quickly and pushing the grate open. I slowly raise my head and, sure enough, there's a black unmarked van waiting for us. *Damn Tomás, you're good.*

As I'm climbing out, the back of the van opens, and I run to it at full speed. We need to get out of here immediately, and I don't want to waste any time. I easily jump in and place Madís on the floor. There's a driver, passenger, and one person in the back. They're all dressed in black, and I can sense that they're also vampires. Without turning on the lights, we speed off as fast as the van will go. I fall back against the wall of the van and breathe a sigh of relief; I relax for a second hoping that the worst is behind us. "We made it, we actually made it." I lightly chuckle as I say this.

The front of the van catches my eye. It's not a normal windshield. The entire front window is covered with screens. Below them are control panels. The driver and passenger are pressing buttons and driving the with levers and touchscreens. I've never seen technology like this.

I pull my eyes away and smile over at Madís, but my relief fades when I notice that their eyes are half open. I rush over to check their pulse, but I can barely detect it. I look up at the vamp in the back with me, who slides over with a black bag; she pulls medical equipment out and starts checking Madís' vitals, "Tomás told us he was close to expiration. V, I've never seen someone this far gone still alive. His pupils are non-reactive—was he conscious when you left the compound?"

I quickly answer, "He was in and out, but he was still talking and moving."

"Did he hit his head while you were carrying him? This can also happen from head trauma." She continues to monitor Madís as she's speaking to me.

I replay our escape, wracking my memory for a moment I might have bumped his head against something. "No, I was so careful with them. They were still interacting right before we left the building."

"The truth is, I've never seen a human make it out of there alive, and nobody has ever studied the long-term effects of constant compulsion on top of everything else their body goes through while in confinement. The place we're taking you to has a doctor on staff, she'll be able to take a better look once we're there." I appreciate how concerned this vamp is as she's checking over Madís.

I'm sitting cross legged, and I've laid his head on my lap. I'm sitting towards the back doors of the van and his legs are stretched out towards the front windshield, his head is pushing up against my stomach. I'm stroking his hair when, suddenly, he starts to convulse, and his eyes roll into his head. "He's having a seizure! Please help him!"

"His vitals are dropping rapidly. I don't think he's going to make it to the holding spot." Then she says the one thing I hoped never to hear. "You need to turn him. It's the only way we can be sure that he'll make it. We're still three hours away from our destination and I have nothing in here to stabilize him."

I shut my eyes tight and shake my head rapidly. *No, no, no it wasn't supposed to be like this. I can't do this to him. I can't force this life on them, I don't want them to turn into this.*

When their body finally stills, I curl down and place my forehead against theirs. I breathe their scent deeply and a vision is triggered.

We're laying in my bed at home in L.A. and we're giggling. "What did you think of me the first time you saw me?" I ask playfully.

"That you were the most gorgeous creature I had ever seen." They say as they stroke my naked shoulder.

"How did you get the nerve to approach me?"

216

"I was drunk, and my friend dared me." They hide their face in the white pillow after this embarrassing revelation.

"Shut the fuck up! Are you serious? Our love story started because of a dare?" I let out a gleeful squeal and climb on top of him. His bare chest makes me tingle and I lower myself to their stomach, eager to taste their skin.

My dream world is ripped away from me just as quickly as it appeared, and I'm back in my nightmare. *That's what we could have had. If I hadn't been so scared of what I was, everything could have been different.*

Tears fall from my eyes into their hair as I whisper, "I'm sorry, Baby Boy. I can't turn you into something that I hate." I lift my head up and gently kiss them on the lips, breathe them in one more time before letting them go.

I say goodbye to the only soul who's ever seen me for all that I am, and who loved me immeasurably despite the darkest parts of myself. I say goodbye to my heart ever feeling whole again. Every encounter I've had with Madís is rushing into my mind. I'm so overwhelmed I can't think clearly. I feel like I can't breathe even though I don't actually need to breathe and I start gagging.

"V, is there anything I can do for you?" The vamp wants to approach me but they're not sure that's a good idea.

I shake my head no, I can't handle being touched right now, everything is too loud. I plug my ears with my fingers, *it wasn't supposed to be like this, it wasn't supposed to be like this....* "Hhhmmmmmm...hhmmmmm...hhmmmmmm..." *I don't know how to fix it, why can't I fix it? Fuuuuuuuck!* Tears are streaming down my face, I'm covering my eyes with my hands, I want to push all my emotions deep down, I want to turn it all off.

As my eyes are closed, I reach deep within me and close the door that holds all of the sadness, all of the love, all of the good I've ever experienced while with Madís.

As I look up at the vamp across from me, the helplessness that they feel is apparent on their face. As "Ava Adore" by **The Smashing Pumpkins** gets triggered and starts to play in my mind my thoughts are clouded with rage, *The Commission has no idea what they've just started...*

Acknowledgement

Ethan, Alice, Nessie, and Adrienne thank you for teaching me how to love life. To my rock, Jeff, I could have never done this without your support. To the loves that are always in my corner Naty, Hilda, Sarah, Rachelle, Chris, Emily, Stephanie, Alyssa, Jenny, Bailey, Sara, Alex, Keir, and Jen. A big thank you to my author support team especially MJ, Poppy, Anastasia, and Abigail.

About The Author

Aura Marquez Lives in Southern California with her 3 kids, husband, 3 dogs, 2 cats, 5 chickens, a fish, and a gecko named Noodles. In middle school she developed a love for reading, and vampires, as a way to cope with the constant bullying that she endured because she was different. As she got more and more into the supernatural genre she longed to see herself in the  make-believe worlds she loves so much. She created V as a love letter to her queer, Chicane, and autistic communities which have shaped the person she is today.

Made in the USA
Las Vegas, NV
11 June 2024